# YULE BE SORRY

## A CHRISTMAS COZY MYSTERY SERIES

### MONA MARPLE

"He's been kidnapped," Mrs Claus informed me with a frown. Her usually bright eyes, often reflecting twinkling Christmas lights, had dulled with sorrow. It made sense if Gilbert was kidnapped.

The sassy but devoted elf that was usually everywhere in Claus Cottage, racing to get guests to the door, serving hot chocolates, making warm meals in the kitchen, and constantly threatening to hang up his apron in some protest or another, wasn't anywhere tonight.

There was a deafening kind of silence that followed the disheartening announcement and Father Christmas' sudden departure to prepare the sleigh. Claus Cottage was the kind of place in Candy Cane Hollow that was always brimming with joy, especially so close to Christmas. Perched atop a snowy hill and outlined with lights and décor, it was hard to think our Christmas here this year would be a slow, quiet one. It would be, without Gilbert.

Tomorrow was Christmas Eve, and I refused to believe we would spend it without dear Gilbert. In that silence, guilt found its way towards my tightening chest. Only half an hour ago, I had seen Gilbert. I shouldn't have left him behind to fetch his measuring cups by himself. I should've come with him. Maybe he'd still be around if I had.

Before I could utter a word, my knees buckled, and a wave of dizziness washed over me; Nick's strong hands grasped my elbow just in time, his touch warm and reassuring. He gently guided me to a nearby settee, the soft cushions sinking slightly under my weight as I sat down, the faint scent of cinnamon and pine enveloping me, providing a brief moment of comfort amidst the chaos. The gold grandfather clock with green garlands and a large red ribbon suddenly rang, breaking the silence. It was midnight, but no one flinched at the sound.

"Oh dear," Mrs Claus raced to my side. "You must be in shock. Nick, call Wiggles and report this, please, while I tend to Holly."

Nick looked torn between rushing to my side and doing as his mum asked, and I gave him a weary smile to show that he should go ahead and make the phone call.

"I... I was just with Gilbert earlier tonight," I explained, as if it would change anything. "After finding Angel, he went back for his measuring cups."

Mrs Claus placed my freezing hands in hers. "You couldn't have known, Holly."

I felt tears pool at the bottom of my eyes as I mumbled, "I should've come with him, or at least waited for him."

"Don't say that," Mrs Claus firmly said. "This is not the time to point fingers, Holly. The only person to blame is the one who took Gilbert."

August, my sister, who had been crying on a nearby chair, sniffed. "Who could've taken Gilbert? Who would do such a thing?"

"Wiggles will sort this out in no time, you watch," Mrs

Claus said, but her voice wobbled and she couldn't quite look at me or August as she spoke.

"But... who could do such a thing?" August asked in between choked tears.

"He has to be safe. He just has to," I murmured. "If anything happens to him, I'll... well, I'll...!"

"We won't let anything happen to him," Mrs Claus insisted.

August let out a bitter laugh. "And how do we stop it when we have no idea where he is. Does he even have any enemies?"

Mrs Claus cocked her head to one side. "Oh, well, nothing serious."

"What does that mean?" I asked, on alert. Gilbert had enemies? Sure, he had his idiosyncrasies, but didn't everyone?

"It's just, well, how can I say this? Elves can be envious," Mrs Claus said with a shrug of her shoulders.

"You mean Gilbert has enemies because he works here," I said as her meaning sank in. "He's at risk because of us!"

"No, no, that's not true, dear. Gilbert has a good job and he can be a little prideful. Not all elves think he should be so open about that pride."

August wailed again from her seat. "And now some maniac has taken him to teach him a lesson!"

Mrs Claus looked down at the carpet in silence, and then I noticed her shoulders gently heaving. She was crying. I found that my own weak emotional resolve couldn't put up any more of a fight, and I gave in to my own tears.

And there the three of us sat, each lost in our own horrid thoughts about where our beloved Gilbert could be and what his captor might do to him.

Before any of us could snap out of the dark mood, the

doorbell rang. We glanced at each other nervously, an ominous feeling setting in as the sound of the doorbell faded.

"I'll get it," Nick called from the hallway, and I was grateful for his chivalry. He must have finished on the phone and was clearly relieved to have another job to do.

A part of me still waited for the sound of Gilbert's little feet shuffling in a hurry from the kitchen so he could get to the door first. He would've scolded Nick if he knew he had dared to open the front door himself. He'd throw a fit, say he must be such a useless elf if he couldn't even be trusted with opening the door. I tried to shake those thoughts away as Nick disappeared to the front door.

But then Nick suddenly gasped, followed by a series of coughs that concerned all of us in the den. Mrs Claus, August, and I hurried to the doorway where we were met by the pungent smell of something earthy and rotten. My hand immediately flew to cover my nose before I threw up the last meal I had enjoyed back at Angel Albright's rental home.

I crept closer to the foul-smelling thing waiting in the front doorway. I immediately realised what it was—a battered leather boot, scuffed and cracked from years of wear, now overflowing with a foul, mushy mass that reeked of spoiled potatoes. The putrid stench hit me like a wall, making my stomach churn as I recoiled from the sight of the decaying, lumpy substance oozing from the boot.

Father Christmas, who was just about to depart with his sleigh, halted abruptly in front of the cottage, his bushy white eyebrows knitting together in curiosity as he took in the unusual commotion. The jingling of the reindeer's harnesses fell silent as he stepped closer, the crisp night air swirling around him, carrying the faint scent of pine and snow.

"Oh no," Father Christmas said with a groan. It appeared that he had immediately recognised the foreign thing on our doorstep. "Is it the 24th of December already?"

Mrs Claus nodded, her hand continuously swatting at the smell as if it was an insect flying before her. "It is, dear. A minute after midnight, to be precise."

Father Christmas looked at the boot with a disapproving gaze. "I completely forgot to renew the contract."

"What contract?" Nick tried not to choke on his own words as he fought off the stench.

"Dasher," Father Christmas turned to the reindeer behind him. "Get back to the shed, will you?"

Then he turned to all of us with a commanding voice. "We better get inside first before that stench nauseates us all."

The five of us headed back inside the den. Even with the front door closed behind Father Christmas, the smell of rotten vegetables still lingered in the air, urging Mrs Claus to bring out an ornament-shaped perfume bottle with an atomiser. She sprayed it into the room, making the space smell like newly-baked gingerbread.

"That should do it," Mrs Claus said as she sat down on the settee beside Father Christmas.

Nick sat beside me, his body pointing to his father as he enquired, "You said something about a contract, didn't you, dad? What does that have to do with a... boot filled with rotten potatoes?"

Father Christmas shook his head, mostly disappointed with himself. I supposed I had never thought I'd get to see the day Santa Claus would be disappointed with himself, yet here I was.

Father Christmas began, "Nick, son, as the current Santa Claus, I should've been more keen on passing down your duties and responsibilities as part of your training. It completely slipped my mind! But there's this contract we as Santas have to renew every ten years. And I just missed the midnight mark for it."

"And so we get an unpleasant gift at our doorway as... a penalty?" Nick asked, confused.

"It's the beginning of a series of more unfortunate tricks, to put it bluntly."

I found myself as equally puzzled as Nick. Did Father Christmas just say 'tricks'? So I asked, "What is that supposed to mean?"

Only Father Christmas could add a daunting tone to an otherwise popular festive song. "It means 'Yule Lads are coming to town'."

I would've laughed if it was any other day—like when Gilbert wasn't missing. But instead, I tried to make sense of what was happening and what Father Christmas was trying to say. Except my brain was high on adrenaline and low on critical thinking. Thankfully, August's wasn't.

She exclaimed in realisation, "Yule Lads? You mean those fictional Icelandic mischievous elves who climb down from their mountain at Christmas and boil children?"

Mrs Claus seemed flustered by August's morbid description as she gasped, "Oh my, no! That sounds a bit too dark. And no, Yule Lads are neither fictional nor Icelandic. They most certainly don't boil children. But they are indeed mischievous."

Father Christmas added, "Yule Lads are actually just troll-like elves. There are thirteen of them living on a mountain at the furthest edge of Candy Cane Hollow. They're... tricksters known to play elaborate pranks in Candy Cane Hollow during Christmastime. Their tricks, however, are quite the nuisance."

Nick quickly pieced everything together as quick as a Santa-in-training should. "That's why you entered into a contract with them? So they won't pull their tricks on the people and elves of Candy Cane Hollow?"

Father Christmas gave a grave nod. "That's right, son. Imagine how annoying it is to deal with pranks at the busiest time of the year."

"But you said the ten-year contract expired at midnight today?"

"Midnight yesterday," I corrected in a faint voice.

"It did—I was completely preoccupied by... Gilbert's kidnapping among other things."

Mrs Claus gently ran her comforting hand along her husband's broad back, her touch soft and soothing against the fabric of his well-worn red coat. The warmth of her hand seemed to pass through the thick material, offering a silent reassurance as she traced small, calming circles with her fingertips. "It couldn't be helped, dear. There's still time to fix this."

"I'll fix it," Nick volunteered.

But Father Christmas had other plans. "No, Nick. I'll fix it; it was me who forgot to renew the contract. Plus, you should be focusing on gift deliveries, shouldn't you?"

Nick groaned, not because he was complaining about gift deliveries at Christmas—the holy grail of Santa activities—but because he wished he could help his dad more. He was a devoted son. It was one of the many things I loved about him.

I reached for my fiancé's hand to ease his worries just as Father Christmas got up from his seat. "I'll fix this right now."

Glancing out the window, I could see the snowfall had doubled compared to ten minutes ago.

Mrs Claus could see the same thing as she pacified her husband. "It's not the right weather to meet the Yule Lads, dear. You can do that first thing in the morning."

Father Christmas calmly argued, "But no weather would stop them from wreaking havoc."

"That's an overstatement, dear. The most the Yule Lads will do is steal a few pans and some baked goods."

"That's true usually, but they haven't been out for a decade! Who knows what they could do?"

Hearing that, my ears suddenly perked in curiosity. What could the Yule Lads do? Was it just impeccable timing that Father Christmas forgot to renew his contract with a bunch of trickster trolls-slash-elves on the same night that Gilbert was kidnapped? Was it just a coincidence or an elaborate prank?

If Father Christmas was right, the Yule Lads might've been kept in their mountain for far too long, and what better way to announce their return than by kidnapping the Claus' house elf before their trademark rotten-potato-filled-boots prank?

It made sense to me. Given the urgent need to find Gilbert and bring him home to Claus Cottage, I pitched the idea to the group before giving it more thought. I didn't want to waste time.

"Is it possible that the Yule Lads took Gilbert as a... joke?" I thought out loud.

"Oh, please, no," Mrs Claus' voice was barely a whisper and she began to cry again.

Father Christmas turned to me, his eyebrows furrowing together in thought as he replied, "It wouldn't be the first time the Yule Lads took someone."

Just then, the doorbell rang again. We all turned our heads in unison, startled by the interruption. Nick went to answer it, and moments later, a familiar face stepped into the room.

"Ethan!" Mrs Claus exclaimed, clearly surprised. "What brings you here at this hour?"

Ethan Evergreen, the owner of Evergreen Emporium, stood in the doorway, looking a bit disheveled and anxious. "I'm sorry to bother you all so late, but I heard some commotion and thought I'd check in. Is everything alright?"

Mrs Claus sighed, "Not exactly, Ethan. Gilbert has been kidnapped, and we suspect the Yule Lads might be involved."

Ethan's eyes widened in genuine concern. "That's terrible! Gilbert is such a wonderful elf. If there's anything I can do to help, please let me know."

"Thank you, Ethan," Mrs Claus said warmly. "We'll certainly let you know if we need anything. Right now, we're just trying to figure out what to do next."

Ethan nodded, then hesitated before speaking again. "I could wait here for Gilbert if you wanted? If you needed a person here, while you search?"

Mrs Claus pouted a little as she took in the offer. "That's very kind, Ethan, but no. Thank you. I know what long hours you're working at the store. You get home and rest, dear."

Ethan seemed disappointed with the response, but turned and waved farewell.

## 2

I couldn't sleep. There was no way I was sleeping again until we found Gilbert. I still felt guilty about letting him go off on his own, but Mrs Claus was right. This wasn't the time for me to engage in self-pity.

We had to find Gilbert, even if it was Christmas Eve. Most especially since it was Christmas Eve. He had to be home to make Christmas dinner – that was just how things were meant to be. Gilbert was meant to cook all meals at Claus Cottage much like Santa had to deliver the presents to boys and girls across the world. That was the natural order of things.

Speaking of Santa, by the time I got out of bed, Nick had already left to oversee the HQ for tonight's Christmas deliveries. Of course, they now had a modern system to deliver gifts. He couldn't possibly do it all by himself, but Nick still had to make sure all the nice kids were getting the gifts on their wish lists. There was also toy quality control, packaging and wrapping, Christmas cards, and mailing addresses to check. It was the busiest time of the year for

Nick and the rest of Candy Cane Hollow. And yet Claus Cottage was idle without Gilbert.

I found myself standing in the middle of the kitchen, the scent of gingerbread and pine still lingering in the air. I imagined Gilbert bustling about, his small frame darting between the stove, where a pot of stew might be bubbling, the fridge, its door ajar as he searched for ingredients, and the semi-dirty sink, piled with dishes he would have scolded us for leaving. His presence filled the room with an energy that was palpably absent, leaving only a hollow silence in its place. It wasn't like Mrs Claus to leave dishes in the sink, but she didn't even have the heart to do anything in Gilbert's space. It felt like a betrayal.

I wanted to let myself cry, but I couldn't. I didn't even think I deserved to cry. All that was left for me to do was to find Gilbert. But first, I had to find the Yule Lads. Where would I even begin?

As if the universe was rooting for me, I heard footsteps emerge from the den. Mrs Claus spoke, "I'll come with you. I have to see Gilbert for myself."

Without further ado, I ran towards the voice, finding Mrs Claus and Father Christmas putting on their coats for an early morning ride. Thankfully, the snow had subsided as much as it was ever likely to in Candy Cane Hollow on Christmas Eve.

"Holly," Mrs Claus chimed. "You're up awfully early."

"I could say the same to you," I remarked. "Are you going to look for Gilbert?"

"We are paying a visit to the Yule Lads."

"I'm coming with you!" I quickly decided, making it apparent that I wouldn't take no for an answer as I hurried up the stairs. "I'll just change into warmer clothes. I'll be down in two seconds!"

Neither Mrs Claus nor Father Christmas had the chance to argue. I rushed to my bedroom and put on warmer clothes under my chunky coat and some boots. By the time I got back downstairs, Mrs Claus was waiting for me so we could ride Father Christmas' sleigh off to, well, I wasn't sure where.

As Mrs Claus placed the fleece blanket over our laps, I asked her, "Do you know where to find these Yule Lads?"

Father Christmas secured everything and ordered the reindeer to go. So we were on our way.

Father Christmas replied from the front seat in Mrs Claus' stead, "We're headed to No Carols Cave – that's where the Yule Lads live."

Mrs Claus added, "It's on the mountain at the very edge of Candy Cane Hollow. A place of unpredictable weather where snow never falls, Christmas lights don't work, and carols are unheard."

"Hence No Carols Cave," I noted.

"That's right. I suggest you hold tight since it's a place unlike any other part of Candy Cane Hollow. We won't know the weather until we get there."

We sleighed past the High Street, where I spotted a large sign in the window of Evergreen Emporium. It was one of few stores with lights already on inside, and I could see a figure moving around inside.

"Does that say what I think it does?" I asked, but the wind meant my words went unheard. We were too high for me to be certain, but the sign in Ethan's window looked awfully as if it was announcing a closing down sale.

We continued on through the town centre and past the reindeer farms. The few people who were out and about all waved at our passing sleigh, greeting us Merry Christmas over and over. My arms grew tingly from all the waving and my voice grew hoarse from all the greeting. Mrs Claus and Father Christmas were used to it and showed no signs of fatigue.

As we rode further, the festive sight of Candy Cane Hollow was replaced by vast sheets of white snow. The cobblestone roads narrowed into winding pathways, which soon diminished into faint, barely visible tracks that twisted and turned through the dense forest. As the tracks faded into the fresh and untouched snow, our sleigh glided silently into a thick, swirling mist. The air grew sharply colder, biting through our warm clothes with an icy chill that was unlike anything I had ever felt in Candy Cane Hollow. The mist enveloped us, its damp, frigid tendrils creeping into every corner of the sleigh, muffling the sound of the reindeers' hooves and cloaking the world in an eerie, otherworldly silence.

After what felt like an eternity in the blinding mist, we emerged into a surreal, frozen meadow. The landscape was a vivid green, reminiscent of a springtime haven, yet the air was filled with the biting chill of winter. Delicate ice encased the blooming flowers, their petals suspended in crystallised beauty, and even the butterflies appeared frozen in mid-flight, their wings glittering like fragile glass. The ground beneath us was covered in what looked like grass, but as the sleigh moved forward, it crunched under the runners with a brittle sound, each blade encased in a thin layer of frost that sparkled in the muted light. The juxtaposition of the vibrant, life-filled scenery and the numbing cold created a hauntingly beautiful, almost magical atmosphere.

The trees didn't shake with the wind—they were frozen in place. A distant river was also frozen. It was like we had entered a meadow stuck inside a freezer. My eyes moved up from the ground, and that was when I saw a gigantic mountain towering over us.

"Brace yourselves," Father Christmas told us as he said, "Up we go, reindeer!"

Mrs Claus held my hand as the sleigh lifted off the ground and ascended towards the mountain. I held my breath as I looked down at the greenery. I realised that the entire magical place was bordered with thick mist, blocking any view of Candy Cane Hollow in the distance. We flew higher and higher until we reached a clear landing right in front of a gaping maw near the top of the mountain. Sharp and jagged rocks surrounded the rocky hillside. Minerals and vegetation grew around the cave.

No Carols Cave. A sloppy sign was placed right by the cave's entrance; *DO NUT ENTER!!!*

"We better get that sign replaced," Mrs Claus muttered under her breath, still dutiful despite this place probably being home to Gilbert's kidnappers.

The cave beckoned me forward. As if whispers of secrets came from the cave's mouth, I stepped towards the entrance, but Father Christmas put a protective arm before me. "I better head in first. Stay close behind me."

I nodded, grateful that Father Christmas was also looking out for me. Mrs Claus and I stayed behind him as he led the way. The cave was only momentarily dark. After a few steps or so, the winding passage reflected light from a fire. I could hear it crackle as we got closer.

As we arrived at the heart of the cave, I was taken aback by the sheer messiness of the place. Gilbert would never have stood for this. The cavernous, hollow space was dimly lit by a bonfire crackling in the centre, its flames casting flickering shadows on the rugged stone walls. Scattered around the fire were rocks of all shapes and sizes, creating uneven seating areas. The floor was littered with rubbish—discarded cups with bent straws, crumpled papers, and grease-stained pastry boxes mingling with various kinds of plastic waste. The air was thick with the smell of burnt wood and old food, a stark contrast to the usually pristine environment of Claus Cottage. The disarray was overwhelming, with piles of trash spilling into corners and stray bits of debris crunching underfoot, creating a chaotic and unsettling atmosphere.

There were precisely thirteen chairs made from twigs and branches and a table made from a tree trunk. In the corner of the cave were ladders. My eyes followed where the ladders led, and there were small caves inside this larger cave. Thirteen smaller caves that I was guessing were the Yule Lads' bedrooms.

"Hello?" Father Christmas bellowed, his voice echoing into the emptiness. "Is anyone home?"

I kept my eyes peeled for horrifying trolls to pop out from one of those caves and maybe ambush us. Since they were tricksters, maybe a paint can would fall on our heads and soak us neon green. Maybe an enclosure on the floor would suddenly open where hungry alligators waited for us to fall with their mouths open. I didn't know what to be nervous about, but I was definitely nervous about something. Clearly, I had no idea what the Yule Lads were like.

"Hello?" Father Christmas tried again.

But as his voice bounced off the walls and warranted no movement or response, it was becoming apparent that the place was empty. Turning to Mrs Claus, I said, "I don't think Gilbert is here."

Mrs Claus sighed. "Well, if they want to use Gilbert as a negotiating tool for the contract, I did think it's doubtful they'd keep him in the most obvious place we could find him."

"You think they'd take Gilbert to help them negotiate?" I asked. Even though I had first raised the suggestion, I didn't want to believe it was true. Poor Gilbert. He must be so scared.

"Judging by this place, I can confidently say they didn't take Gilbert to do their chores."

I couldn't agree more. As I continued looking around, the space suddenly echoed with a growl that made my skin crawl. Was there another creature in here?

Father Christmas gestured for us to stay behind him, his broad frame a reassuring barrier as we waited anxiously for the creature to emerge from the depths of one of the smaller caves. The suspense was palpable, every second stretching endlessly. Finally, a massive black figure with four powerful legs and a sinuous, sweeping tail slinked out of the shadows. My breath caught in my throat as I watched in horror, each deliberate step echoing through the cavern. It moved with a predatory grace, its movements slow and menacing as it pounced onto the ground before us. When it fully emerged into the light of the bonfire, I realised with a jolt of terror that it was a colossal black cat, easily as large as an elephant. Its sharp yellow eyes glowed with an eerie intensity, glaring at us with a mix of curiosity and thinly veiled menace. The creature's fur was sleek and dark, absorbing the flickering light, and its massive paws made no sound as it approached, heightening the surreal and terrifying nature of the encounter.

"Stand back, kitty," Father Christmas extended his arm towards the cat. "We're just here to talk to the Yule Lads. Do you know where they are?"

In Candy Cane Hollow, talking to animals wasn't a

strange occurrence. After all, reindeer could talk, so why wouldn't an abnormally large cat?

For a tense moment, Father Christmas and the enormous cat locked eyes in a silent, unblinking stare-off. The air was thick with anticipation, and I could feel my heart pounding in my chest. The cat's piercing yellow eyes seemed to bore into Father Christmas, its tail twitching slightly as if contemplating its next move.

"I take it you're Frostwhisker?" Father Christmas asked as the cat reared back as if ready to attack. His words caused the enormous kitty to freeze in place.

The cat hissed then raised a front leg and licked its paw. "Who's asking?"

The cat's voice was velvety smooth and hypnotising and I found that I couldn't stop watching its huge frame.

"You know very well who I am. What do you think you're doing behaving in such a way to the Claus family?"

Frostwhisker batted long black eyelashes over her bright green eyes. "I'm a guard cat. This is my job. Don't like it? Take it up with my owners."

I gasped involuntarily. I had never imagined any person or creature would have such an attitude towards Father Christmas.

"I'll be happy to! Where are they? And do they always leave their home in such a mess or did they leave in a hurry?"

Frostwhisker sat down and began to scratch behind an ear. "They don't answer to me."

Father Christmas turned his face a fraction and addressed Mrs Claus and I. "This is pointless. No wonder this cat is on the naughty list."

Frostwhisker let out a piercing cry as if he had been wounded. "I'm on the what?"

Father Christmas gave us a wink as the cat's demeanour shifted dramatically. It lowered itself onto its stomach, the massive body relaxing into a more familiar, feline posture. With a surprising gentleness, it nudged its head against Father Christmas' outstretched hand, a deep, resonant purr vibrating through the cavern. The sound was both soothing and surreal, given the cat's immense size.

Father Christmas chuckled softly, scratching behind the creature's ears as if it were a common house cat. The transformation was so abrupt and complete that I let out a relieved breath I hadn't realised I'd been holding. It was just like any other domesticated cat, only a thousand times bigger. Phew.

"You're not so bad after all, hmm. Now, tell me, has anyone new been around in this cave since yesterday?" Father Christmas asked as he petted the giant feline. I found myself chuckling at the sight but soon stopped when it became evident that Gilbert wasn't there. And neither were the Yule Lads. Where were they?

"Nobody ever comes here apart from the thirteen," Frostwhisker purred.

"Very well," Father Christmas said with sad resignation. "I'll be sure to make the HW aware of your help, Frost-whisker."

As we returned to the sleigh, ready to head back to Claus Cottage, we were all lost in our own thoughts. The journey home flashed by in an instant, I was so distracted by contemplating where Gilbert could be.

"What's going on here?" Father Christmas asked as we finally flew over Claus Cottage. A small crowd had gathered on the front lawn.

As we climbed out of the sleigh and approached,

someone I recognised dashed across the snow towards us. It was Beatrice Birch, the owner of Birch's Books.

"Do you have news?" I called, unable to hide the hope in my voice.

"Oh!" Beatrice exclaimed as she covered her mouth with her hand. "No, no, I'm sorry. I heard about Gilbert and thought I'd join the search. Any luck so far?"

I shook my head, feeling grateful for the support but overwhelmed by the growing crowd. "No, we didn't find anything yet."

"Ethan said you thought the Yule Lads are behind it. I've read so much about them over the years. But kidnap, really?"

As we all pondered Beatrice's words, Oliver Pine, the owner of Pine's Pastries, walked across with a concerned expression. "I thought I'd offer my help. Gilbert's disappearance has us all worried."

I noticed Ethan Evergreen peering into the den window.

"Ethan?" I called out, surprised to see him again so soon. "What are you doing here?"

Ethan hurried over, his face flushed from the cold and a look of concern on his face. "I couldn't stop thinking about Gilbert. There must be something I can do to help. Even... well, I can clean?"

Mrs Claus gave him a warm, albeit puzzled, smile. "That's very kind of you, Ethan. But we're not worried about the cleaning. Gilbert is part of the family."

Ethan sighed, looking disappointed. "Of course. Well, I'll be going. I guess. Unless there's anything at all I can do to help. Anything."

Father Christmas nodded appreciatively. "Thank you all for your concern and willingness to help. If you hear or see anything suspicious, please let us know immediately. We need all the help we can get."

Mrs Claus gave a heavy sigh. "Since we already have the sleigh ready, dear, shall we take a quick fly over town and see if we can spot anything?"

"Yes!" I agreed.

"Good idea," Father Christmas said, and with a quick flick of the reins, we ascended again.

**3**

As we flew low over Candy Cane Hollow, even in our dejected stupor, it was clear that something was different. The usually bustling streets were eerily subdued, and everyone seemed too preoccupied to wave and greet us with the usual hearty Merry Christmas. Although it was expected that everyone would be busy on Christmas Eve, even the word 'busy' felt different. Something had happened.

The first sign of trouble was an elf crying over at his yew tree farm. Dozens of yew trees had been plucked and chewed on. Next, we saw the milk-elf frantic over crates of spoiled milk, bottles either empty or half-consumed. As we moved further into town, people and elves rushed in and out of the grocery store, panic-buying cans of whipped cream, sausages, and meat. A long line snaked outside the patisserie, where customers demanded pastries and baked goods from the overwhelmed baker and his wife.

"Goodness gumdrops," I muttered under my breath.

Even the candy store had closed early, its shelves ransacked. Mrs Claus asked Father Christmas to stop in front of the grocery store. She stepped down from the sleigh and called everyone's attention. "Everyone! What on Christmas Eve's travesty is happening here?"

Despite the panic, they couldn't possibly ignore Mrs Claus. For a moment, they all calmed down and gathered around the sleigh.

An elf with bags of whipped cream in her arms complained, "Someone emptied all the whipped cream in my kitchen! How am I supposed to make hot chocolates without it?"

Another person chimed in, "I prepared meat and sausages for my relatives who are coming to town today, but when I woke up this morning, they were all either bitten or stolen!"

A clamour followed those comments from other people and elves who had all experienced the same thing that morning.

I joined Mrs Claus, listening to the multitude of complaints.

"Someone stole my pots and pans!"

"Someone ate half of my breakfast casserole straight out of the pan!"

"I awoke to someone incessantly stomping on my roof!"

"Someone is slamming all our doors and opening the windows!"

"A thief took off with my pies and cakes!"

"Someone took all my children's Christmas candies!"

The loudest voice by far, however, was familiar to my ears, and I looked through the crowd until I saw who it belonged to. There, face red as Rudolph's nose and with deep worry lines etched on his forehead, was Ethan Evergreen.

"Ethan?" I called to him as Mrs Claus listened to a whole catalogue of complaints from the rest of the crowd.

Ethan seemed surprised to see me, almost as if he had reached a point of hysteria. "Holly. I'm sorry."

"No, don't apologise. You sounded really upset. What's happened?"

He shook his head in an attempt to appear calm, but his bushy eyebrows were furrowed with worry.

"Please. You've been so thoughtful to all of us worried about Gilbert. Maybe I can help you."

Ethan let out a long, shaky breath. "I've been victim to the same cruel tricks as everyone else in town. They've turned my store upside down. I'd... I'd been up all night sorting through stock and my displays. Then I just popped across to Claus Cottage and now it's all ruined."

My heart sank for the poor man. "Ethan, I'm so sorry. I'll be happy to help you tidy up, just as soon as we've found Gilbert."

Ethan opened his mouth in a perfect little circle, the very picture of someone shocked. "Holly, who is at Claus Cottage right now?"

"Well," I considered the question. I knew that August was taking baby Jeb to a reindeer farm for the morning, and Tom would be busy at Santa HQ, as would Nick. "Nobody."

A smile - no, a grimace - crossed Ethan's face. "You absolutely mustn't leave Claus Cottage empty, Holly. Not with this madness going on."

"But we need to be out searching for Gilbert," I countered.

He nodded his agreement. "You do, you're right. Oh, if only there was someone who could - wait, I can do it! I can stay at Claus Cottage and keep guard."

"We really couldn't expect you to do such a thing. Not

with the mess you say your store is in. Don't you need to get it sorted?"

"I'll do that later. We're closed tomorrow in any event and I have no plans, so I can sort it all then. I insist, Holly, please let me do this for you."

"Okay," I agreed. "And please, make yourself at home. The kitchen is full of food and drink. Gilbert always makes sure of that."

The mention of Gilbert reminded me of our mission, and I turned my attention from Ethan, who was already heading off towards Claus Cottage.

Overlapping complaints and mumbled agreements filled the air. Mrs Claus had to raise her voice. "Alright! Alright! Everyone, I understand this is a stressful time for all of us, but I ask you not to let this ruin our Christmas. Remember the essence of Christmas: love and generosity!"

The crowd went silent, nodding in understanding, slightly ashamed of their behaviour.

"Now," Mrs Claus clapped her hands once, "Father Christmas is going to fix this matter as quickly as possible. Let us not instil unnecessary fear and worry in each other. As for the missing pies, I'll personally see to it that each household who had a pie stolen receives a Claus mince pie!"

A cheer erupted.

Mrs Claus led me back to the sleigh and nodded to Father Christmas to get the reindeer going as she turned to the crowd. "That's all for now!"

I couldn't help but admire Mrs Claus' love and dedication to the people and elves of Candy Cane Hollow. Despite the stressful situation, she had once again come up with an excellent solution to ease the people's worries. There was no doubt in my mind that I wouldn't be able to fill the big shoes she'd leave me with once she retired as Mrs Claus. But right now, being the next Mrs Claus was the least of my concerns.

As the sleigh moved again, Father Christmas let out a heavy exhale. "The Yule Lads have begun with their practical jokes already. On Christmas Eve!"

Mrs Claus reached forward and squeezed Father Christmas' shoulder. "Surely they're still somewhere around town. We'll find them."

Still dumbfounded, I asked again, "So this is what the Yule Lads do? Steal pans, eat people's food, and stomp on roofs?"

Father Christmas replied, "That's the most basic things they could do." He began to enumerate the Yule Lads. "Clod suckles on farmer's yews. Gully steals cow milk. Stubby steals food straight out of the pan. Spoon licks, well, spoons! Scraper steals pots and pans. Bowie finds hidden food and takes it. Slammer stomps on roofs and slams doors. Gobbler gobbles up whipped cream. Swiper steals sausages. Peeper leaves windows open. Hook snatches up all the meat he can find. Masher steals potatoes and stomps on them until they make an awful stench. Finally, Candy steals candies."

I took a moment to process all the names and pranks, even though I could barely remember all thirteen of them. I replied, "What's the worst they could do? Kidnap elves? Like Gilbert?"

Father Christmas cleared his throat. "I'll take you ladies home for now so you can make those mince pies. It'll be quite the job without Gilbert around. I'll gather the Yule Lads myself."

I didn't dare protest, sensing that something else was troubling Father Christmas. His usually merry eyes were clouded with worry, and a deep furrow creased his forehead. The jovial twinkle that typically accompanied his every move was noticeably absent, replaced by a heavy, contemplative air. I could feel the tension radiating from him, an unspoken burden that weighed heavily on his broad shoulders.

Before we knew it, Father Christmas had pulled over in front of Claus Cottage. Mrs Claus gave Father Christmas a kiss on the cheek before joining me at the door. "Take care, my dear."

"I will," Father Christmas uttered with a gruff expression.

As soon as Mrs Claus was beside me, the sleigh took off again, not wasting a minute longer.

I had forgotten all about Ethan being at Claus Cottage until we arrived back there and saw that the front door had been left wide open.

"Ethan!" I cried as I ran in the doorway, worried that the Yule Lads had come back and taken him as well.

There was a clattering from down the hall and then the small door to Gilbert's room opened. Ethan came into view and gave us an awkward wave and a smile.

"Ethan, what on Santa's sleigh are you doing in Gilbert's room?" Mrs Claus asked.

"Forgive me!" He cried. "I only wanted to try and help. I figured while I was housesitting I could look for clues. You know, bring a fresh pair of eyes to the investigation."

Mrs Claus frowned. "That's very kind, dear, but Gilbert really is particular about his privacy."

"Of course. Of course. I just... well, if there was a kidnap note or anything... I..." Ethan stammered.

"There was a kidnap note, yes," Mrs Claus said. "Chief Superintendent Wiggles has it and is probably examining it as we speak."

Ethan gave out a small squeak. "That's good. I'm pleased that's all in hand."

"Thank you for your help, Ethan. Don't let us keep you from your store," I said, and he gave me a slightly maniacal grin and virtually ran past us and out into the snow.

I looked at Mrs Claus and tried to read her thoughts, but her well practiced poker face gave nothing away.

"Is he okay?" I asked her finally.

She shook her head sadly. "I worry for him. Evergreen Emporium has been in his family for generations. It's a lot of pressure on his shoulders."

I considered telling Mrs Claus about the sign I was sure I'd seen in his shop window, but I decided not to. I didn't know what the purpose would be of sharing such news, and I didn't want to gossip about others' misfortune.

A silence grew between Mrs Claus and me until we dutifully headed to the kitchen. We didn't want to touch the space but had to since at least a hundred mince pies needed to be baked. Thankfully, my sister, who knew her way around a kitchen much better than I did, appeared.

August could see that Mrs Claus seemed troubled as she dusted her workplace with flour to start baking her famous mince pies. She pulled me aside. "I'm guessing you didn't find Gilbert yet?"

My heart sank. "Unfortunately, no. We went to where the Yule Lads live, but they weren't there – they've already started their pranks around town, and it's causing quite the mess!"

"Well, where could they be keeping Gilbert?"

"I have no idea, sis."

"Are you sure it was them who took him?"

"Who else?" I wondered. "It's been eight hours since they took Gilbert!"

August paused to think. "No one just gets kidnapped for no reason. I'm sure someone will call with more information."

"I hope so." I glanced at Mrs Claus, who seemed distracted as she worked on the pies' pastry, her hands moving mechanically, absent-mindedly smoothing the dough. Her usual gentle hum was absent, replaced by a furrowed brow and distant gaze, lost in thought. The warm, spicy aroma of mince filling contrasted sharply with the worry etched on her face.

"We're making mince pies for the town. Do you think you could help us?" I asked August.

She nodded. "Definitely. Your wonderful Nick has insisted that Tom take the rest of the day off. He'll be happy to have some time alone with Jeb."

Instead of gushing about my fiancé some more as I'd usually be more than happy to, August and I joined Mrs Claus in the kitchen. I hoped that baking would be therapeutic for Mrs Claus, who was missing Gilbert.

As I stood awkwardly awaiting a job, I heard a crash from the pantry and dashed in there. The small space was impeccably organised, of course, and I couldn't see that anything had fallen from the shelves. Then I noticed a small stone on the floor and felt a gust of wind race in through the frosted glass window. As I looked up at the window, I saw a shape outside move quickly out of view.

"There's someone out there!" I cried, and I dashed to the front door and out into the snow in just my socks and slippers. I trudged around the whole perimeter of the house but there was nobody to see, and the snow was falling so heavily it was impossible to see any footprints after more than a moment or two.

August caught up with me and grabbed my arm. "What

the heck are you doing, sis? We've already got one person kidnapped, don't make it two! You don't run to danger!"

Her words hit me and I began to shake, no doubt with a mix of the cold and the realisation of the risk I had just taken. Someone - or something - had broken the pantry window and I had raced off after them without a thought for my safety. Or for August or Mrs Claus, who would of course run after me. I had put us all in danger.

I hung my head in shame. "I'm sorry."

August pulled me close and led me back to Claus Cottage, where we ensured that all of the doors and windows were locked. Mrs Claus called Wiggles to report the incident, but the call went to voicemail.

"Let's get back to baking. It's the best thing I know to settle my nerves," Mrs Claus suggested.

The kitchen soon filled with the comforting scents of nutmeg, cloves, and cinnamon as we worked. August expertly rolled out the pastry dough, her movements precise and practiced. Mrs Claus, though distracted, deftly cut out circles of dough, placing them gently into the waiting pie tins. I mixed the rich, fruity mince filling, the blend of dried fruits and spices creating a vibrant mosaic in the bowl. The warmth from the oven enveloped us, a stark contrast to the cold worry gnawing at our hearts. The pies, once assembled, were placed in the oven, and we watched as the crusts turned a perfect golden brown, the filling bubbling gently. The rhythmic process of baking brought a momentary peace; a brief respite from our concerns.

One batch of mince pies later, the doorbell rang.

"I'll get it!" I volunteered as I wiped my floury fingers on my apron and jogged toward the front door.

I felt nervous as I put my hand around the doorknob. "Please be Gilbert," I prayed under my breath.

As the front door swung open, an elf stood on the other side. But it wasn't Gilbert. This one was female, her bright green work jumpsuit contrasting sharply with the white snow outside. Her red cat-eye glasses sparkled in the soft light from the hallway, framing keen, intelligent eyes. She wore red, pointed boots that looked both sturdy and stylish, each step leaving a neat imprint in the fresh snow on the doorstep. Her expression was a mix of determination and warmth, a reassuring presence amidst the chaos.

"Uh, can I help you?" I asked.

The female elf offered a folder to me. "Holly Wood, is that right? My name's Gwen. I'm from Elf Employment. We've heard about Gilbert's disappearance, so I've been sent here as the new elf assigned to Claus Cottage. Nice to meet you."

Before I could say anything, Gwen moved into the gap in the door and beamed at me.

## 4

_____

I blinked at Gwen, stupefied. "I'm not sure what I can do for you…"

"Mrs Claus will know," Gwen slipped in behind me, pointing to the den. "Is it this way?"

I ran after Gwen, who quickly positioned herself on the settee. She placed two folders on the coffee table before her, ensuring they were both perfectly symmetrical, then smoothed her clothes with her hand. She was acting as if she was here for a scheduled interview.

I withheld a gasp of disbelief and cleared my throat. I knew that I was far from fully up-to-speed with the inner workings of Candy Cane Hollow, but I couldn't believe that Mrs Claus would want to replace Gilbert. "I'll fetch Mrs Claus."

I made my way to the kitchen. Mrs Claus was preparing the second batch of pastries for the mince pies. "Who was at the door, dear?"

"Uh…" I hesitated, unsure of what to say. "She says she's Gwen from Elf Employment."

Mrs Claus flinched, seemingly aware of who our unexpected guest was. Swiftly, she removed her apron and headed straight to the den. Glancing at August in confusion, she and I followed Mrs Claus.

"Mrs Claus." Gwen hopped out of her seat and offered her small hand for a shake. "Nice to see you again."

Mrs Claus shook Gwen's hand and nodded for her to sit as she did the same. August and I also joined them on a separate settee.

Gwen took a deep breath before beginning an elevator pitch that seemed well-rehearsed. "My name's Gwen and I'm from Elf Employment. I'm here to offer my services as the new house elf of Claus Cottage effective immediately. I am skilled in—"

"There must be a mistake." Mrs Claus spoke firmly, interrupting her. "We don't need another house elf. Gilbert will be back, I guarantee you."

Gwen sat with her back straight as an arrow, her eyes squinting despite her thick glasses. She remained unfazed even though she had been interrupted. "I understand why you think that way, Mrs Claus. Of course, I would feel the same if my elf suddenly disappeared on me."

"No, no. Gilbert didn't disappear on us—he was taken."

"Really?" Gwen asked with raised eyebrows.

Mrs Claus gave a firm nod. "The police are investigating and they'll return him very soon."

"Either way, he's proven himself to be undependable."

August and I watched Mrs Claus and Gwen closely. There was clearly tension brewing between them as Mrs Claus remained resolute that Claus Cottage didn't need a new house elf and Gwen insisted otherwise.

At the back of my mind, I could already hear Gilbert's voice threatening us with a hanging apron if he could see this scene. He wouldn't have permitted another elf to seek employment at Claus Cottage. He would chase Gwen out of the premises with a broom if he had to.

Maybe *I* should chase Gwen out with a broom.

From where I sat, I could see tears forming at the bottom of Mrs Claus' eyes. The thought of Gilbert's absence hung heavy in the room. Before a tear could fall on her cheeks, Mrs Claus abruptly stood up from the settee. "Please excuse me, Gwen. Holly will see you out."

Just like that, Mrs Claus exited the room. I could feel my ribs constricting. Mrs Claus' high emotions made it harder to hide my own. I wondered whether I should give Chief Superintendent Wiggles a call. He must've heard something by now.

In the meantime, I returned my attention to Gwen. "I hope you understand how difficult this is for Mrs Claus and all of us. Gilbert is family, and we can't replace family."

Gwen nodded and offered me a smile.

For a second, I thought that would be the end of it all, but then Gwen opened her folder and slid a document over to me. I glossed over the page on the coffee table and read the header: Elf Employment Service Contract Agreement.

I continued reading further and saw that it was a service agreement between the Claus family and Elf Employment stating that in the event of any absence of any house elf for any reason, Elf Employment would immediately provide a new elf to attend to the Claus family's needs.

It didn't make sense to me. I couldn't imagine Mrs Claus hiring private contractors to work at Claus Cottage. Not when she had loyal Gilbert all this time.

I hid my confusion. "I'm not sure when this was signed, but I'm sure Elf Employment could make an exception. We're not going to replace Gilbert."

"It's not really a choice, Holly," Gwen stated matter-of-factly. "It's practically tradition since time immemorial that elves are supposed to serve the Claus family no matter what. It's not even about this agreement; it's about the sacred bond between elves and the Clauses. We live to serve the Clauses, and leaving Claus Cottage devoid of an elf in service? Treasonous!"

Gwen seemed like the kind of elf who strictly followed instructions. I was sure that whatever argument I used, she would have a by-the-book answer. Still, I had to try. We already had too much on our plates: Gilbert's kidnapping, the Yule Lads, the mince pies... I had to get Gwen out of our hair as soon as I could.

"Gwen, is there someone from Elf Employment, perhaps a manager, that I can speak to? Surely we could come up with a compromise."

"It's a holiday; corporate's closed until December 26."

"Oh... then how come you're here?"

"I'm an elf-in-waiting. I'm always on stand-by in case Claus Cottage requires my assistance."

"But I'm telling you we don't need your assistance. Gilbert will be here soon."

"Then I'll just stay until he returns."

"We don't know when that will be..." I groaned, seeing how pointless this conversation was.

August could sense my frustration despite my outwardly calm demeanour. She interjected with an authoritative tone. "Look, Gwen, we appreciate your devotion to Elf Employment and the Clauses, but this is not the best time for us to argue about accepting your services."

I was grateful that my sister was more confrontational than I was, or this conversation would've dragged on between Gwen and I for who knows how long.

August stood up from her seat and pointed her hands towards the doorway. "Should I walk you out?"

Gwen stared at August blankly, like she didn't hear her. Then she turned her gaze to me. "Does this have something to do with my credentials, Holly? Because I can assure you I have the knowledge, experience, and skills to serve the Clauses. Just look at my file!"

This time Gwen handed me the other folder she had prepared.

For the sake of getting Gwen to stop arguing, I accepted the folder and idly flicked through. It was impressive, for sure. Gwen had certificates in Military Precision Bed Making, Organic Cookery 101 right through to 501, Calligraphy, a Masters in Deep Cleaning, and even Diction & Elocution. I handed the folder back and gave her a resigned smile. "It has nothing to do with your credentials, Gwen. You're clearly very accomplished. We're just not going to replace Gilbert."

Gwen's eyes darted from me to August.

At that point, August crossed her arms over her chest and stared at Gwen impatiently. Gwen probably didn't want to risk being carried out of the room because she huffed her chest and turned for the front door.

Before leaving, she said, "I wouldn't want to report this as workplace discrimination, Holly. That wouldn't be a good look for the Clauses."

My eyes widened in shock. "What? We're not discriminating against you at all!"

"It seems like it, given how you wouldn't even give me a chance because... I'm a woman!"

Gwen marched towards the front door, and August saw to it that she did indeed exit the house, leaving me astounded by her accusations of gender discrimination.

But as August returned with a relieved expression on her face, I was just glad that Gwen was no longer here.

"Now that's an elf I wouldn't see eye to eye with," August remarked.

"Tell me about it," I chuckled.

"It's a joke. Get it? I mean because she's too short for me to see eye to eye with, and she seemed like a real pain too."

I rolled my eyes. "Yes, I got it. The jokes generally work better if you don't explain them."

"Just making sure you're on the right wavelength to understand my comedy genius!"

My eyes lingered on the space Mrs Claus had occupied minutes ago before disappearing with tears in her eyes. So I said to August, "You know what, sis? How about you continue those mince pies? I'll go check on Mrs Claus."

August agreed. "You really should. She doesn't seem like herself since Gilbert was kidnapped."

I made my way to Mrs Claus' bedroom, nervous about interrupting her during this emotional time. But I was more adamant that I couldn't leave her by herself. So I gently rapped on her bedroom door.

"Mrs Claus, it's me," I called out from the other side. "Are you okay?"

The first few seconds were quiet, and then she hollered, "Come in, dear! I'm just powdering my nose."

I knew she wasn't powdering her nose—more like blowing her nose after crying.

I pushed the door open and was welcomed by the spacious bedroom, its white bedsheets crisp and inviting. A Christmas-themed quilt, adorned with intricate patterns of snowflakes and holly, lay neatly on top of the duvet, complemented by red and green throw pillows that added a festive touch. The room was bathed in a soft, diffused light from the surrounding windows, their thin curtains embroidered with delicate, hand-sewn snowflakes. On the opposite wall, a shelf stretched from floor to ceiling, filled with Christmas books, their spines worn from years of reading. Next to them, Christmas CDs and signed vinyl records shimmered under the glow of a nearby lamp. Among them, snow globes and figurines of various sizes captured scenes of wintry wonderlands, each one a tiny, frozen moment of joy.

I found Mrs Claus sitting in front of her vanity mirror, actually powdering her nose. "Did you see Gwen out?"

I nodded. "August did. Needless to say, she was... insistent."

"Almost all elves are, Holly. Just like Gilbert bringing all his personal kitchenware everywhere we go!"

I thought I heard Mrs Claus chuckle, so I did the same. But I swallowed it back when I saw Mrs Claus' expression from the mirror's reflection fall.

A prayer escaped her lips. "I hope he's okay."

I crossed the room and crouched down beside Mrs Claus to hold her hand. "We'll find him no matter what, Mrs Claus. Maybe Father Christmas is already on his way here with Gilbert and the Yule Lads."

Mrs Claus offered me a small, sad smile. "I'd like that. But if there's one thing I know about those Yule Lads, it's that they're hard to catch."

With her free hand, Mrs Claus patted my hand before standing up from her chair. "Now, where were we on those mince pies?"

I followed Mrs Claus out of the bedroom. My stomach churned at the thought of our painstakingly slow progress in finding Gilbert.

As Mrs Claus turned to the kitchen, I stayed behind in the hallway to give Wiggles a call.

After four rings, Wiggles picked up. "Hello?"

"Wiggles! It's Holly," I spoke on the phone. "I know it's Christmas Eve, but I was hoping we could get together and talk about... Gilbert."

"Of course! There's no such thing as crime-free holidays! At least, not anymore." Wiggles cleared his throat. "Mrs Claus must be out of her senses! I know how much she loved that dear elf. I'll be there before you know it. Just listen for..."

"*Last Christmas* blasting on your car's speaker, I know," I finished his sentence for him.

## 5

B efore I could even see Wiggles' tiny Fiat, I could already hear the muffled music playing from his car – his favourite song, *Last Christmas,* forever on repeat.

Mrs Claus was so busy putting pies into the oven that she didn't hear Wiggles arriving at Claus Cottage. Not until the doorbell rang, and I left the kitchen to get it.

"Wiggles!" I said a little bit too excitedly, noticing his friend, Cornelius, beside him, "...and Cornelius! Thank heavens you're both here. Come on in."

"Merry Christmas, Holly!" Wiggles greeted.

"You've got some flour on your cheek." Cornelius pointed out.

Wiping my cheek with the ends of my apron, I led them to the settee. "Merry Christmas to you both. But I'm not sure merry is the right word for this year's Christmas Eve."

"Is that Chief Superintendent Wiggles!?" Mrs Claus rushed out of the kitchen as she heard and recognised the voice coming from the den. Upon seeing Wiggles, relief and fear crossed Mrs Claus' expression. "Oh, goodness. Do you have some news for us on Gilbert?"

August appeared behind Mrs Claus and saw that we had guests. "I'll go make some hot chocolates."

"Thank you, dear," Mrs Claus muttered, joining Wiggles and Cornelius. "So, tell me, have you found Gilbert?"

Wiggles slowly shook his head. "I'm afraid there's little progress. In fact, it's almost the same as the information we relayed to you last night – he disappeared fifteen minutes before midnight. Angel Albright made the call when Gilbert didn't show up after he said he'd pick up some ingredients to make vegan burgers as a midnight snack for Angel and her kids."

Cornelius mumbled. "And Lil Bo Cheep."

"Lil Bo Cheep?" Mrs Claus echoed.

I explained. "He's the rapper that one of Angel's daughters is married to. It's not that important."

Cornelius, who loved any opportunity to name drop a famous person or otherwise tell an elaborate story, cleared his throat as if in objection.

"Well, let's get to the important details, Wiggles." Mrs Claus insisted. "Are there any new developments on the search at all?"

"Why, of course," Wiggles replied. "Earlier this morning, we were able to locate where Gilbert was kidnapped."

"Where?" Mrs Claus and I said in chorus.

"Well, right on the High Street! After he bought some ingredients from the only 24-hour grocery in town, All Day Holiday."

I stared at Wiggles. "And...?"

Cornelius responded. "We're going to retrieve security footage of the kidnapping after our visit here."

"What?" I felt slightly ashamed to have called them

during their police work. "You should've told me that over the phone! That seems far too important to delay. Let's go, I'll come with you."

Wiggles and Cornelius didn't get up from their seats.

Instead, Wiggles said. "But the hot chocolates..."

"August!" I hollered. "We'll take the hot chocolates to go!"

Soon, I sat in the backseat of Wiggles' tiny Fiat with a takeout cup in hand, complete with the Claus emblem stamped on the cup sleeve. Wiggles and Cornelius looked like they'd been forced into the front of the tiny vehicle, but neither complained.

I finished my hot chocolate, savouring the last sweet, velvety sip as we pulled up in front of the All Day Holiday store. At first glance, it looked like a simple grocery store, but it was decked out in festive cheer with vibrant splashes of red, green, and white emblazoned everywhere. Twinkling fairy lights framed the windows, casting a warm glow on the falling snow outside. You'd think it was a small store with just two aisles, but as I stepped inside, I realised the aisles stretched far back, seemingly endless, with alphabetically displayed items. Shelves were laden with everything from Christmas-themed pantry staples to specialty holiday treats, the air filled with the mingling scents of peppermint, pine, and fresh-baked gingerbread. It was a wonderland of festive delights, each section meticulously organised and brimming with holiday spirit.

Right away, Cornelius was distracted with moisturisers and face creams – I wouldn't have guessed they would take his interest, but I had long ago learned that Cornelius was surprising in many ways. So, Wiggles and I headed to the back office to retrieve the security footage from last night.

A cheerful young elf with thick glasses that made his

eyes look bigger than normal welcomed us. "Merry Christmas! It has been quite the busy Christmas Eve, huh?"

I glanced back to the aisle where all the baked goods had been bought or taken or ransacked. That and the candies. The aftermath of the Yule Lads' playful schemes.

I wondered if Father Christmas had already gathered them.

"Merry Christmas to you, too," Wiggles replied. "We're here to get the security footage from last night's kidnapping."

"Sure, sure…" the young elf mumbled, jumping into the office chair that was too big for him. "I got it ready and saved it on this flash drive."

The elf handed the flash drive to Wiggles, and Wiggles was content with that, about to nod dismissively. But I stopped him. "Wait, Wiggles. I don't think you've told me how you knew Gilbert was abducted around here?"

The elf answered. "Oh, I made the call. You see, I do my due diligence and watch footage from the night before each one of my morning shifts. At first, I did it for fun, but now, it's become a habit. With the self-checkout and all, it's a good way to pass the time. I didn't realise it was anything much until I heard people talking about that elf of yours who went missing."

I never thought watching security footage was fun, habitual, and a good way to pass the time, but elves could be enthusiastic about some odd things. And in this case, I was extremely grateful for this particular elf's very particular interests.

"You did the right thing," Wiggles told him, and the elf puffed up in pride.

"Do you think we could talk to the night shift employee?" I wondered.

"There's no night shift employee," he explained. "Again, with the self-checkout counter, there's no need. In the case of naughty little kleptomaniacs, the store automatically closes all exit points once someone tries to get past the door without paying. It saves my boss quite the money on wages!"

He really did seem enthusiastic about his job.

"Oh," I couldn't hide my disappointment; an eyewitness might just help us. But on the bright side, there was the security footage. "Well, at least we have the footage."

"Yeah..." the elf chuckled awkwardly. "It might not be much, but yeah."

At first, I didn't understand what the hardworking elf's awkward chuckle meant, but upon arriving at Candy Cane Custody and watching the security footage in Wiggles' office, it finally made sense.

The footage wouldn't be much help because more than half of the camera's lens had been obstructed by snow.

Barely a fraction of the video camera's view could actually be seen. It did, however, catch the precise moment when Gilbert stepped out of All Day Holiday with a bag of ingredients in tow.

I peered closer at the screen – or at least what could be seen from it, and watched Gilbert's legs stop at the edge of the pavement as a black car approached and pulled over in front of him.

Since the camera view was mainly snow, none of us could see the car's make, license plate, or even attempt to identify the person behind the wheel. But after a few seconds of what seemed like a conversation, Gilbert appeared to jump in alarm before getting inside the car in a hurry as if he was threatened to do so.

As the car sped off, the blur of the undecipherable license plate passed the camera frame.

Wiggles concluded. "It seems like a black car took Gilbert!"

And that was all we really had.

Still, I refused to quit. "Wiggles, can you send me a list of all the registered black vehicles here in Candy Cane Hollow?"

I had my doubts about the kidnapper's vehicle being registered with Candy Cane Hollow's DVLA counterpart, but I had to take my chances. Perhaps it was a spontaneous idea. Maybe the Yule Lads stole a car last night. Maybe they even owned one and registered it!

I had dialled a total of 26 out of 42 of the contact numbers for owners of registered black vehicles, always starting with the same joyous tone of "Merry Christmas!" before proceeding to, "I hope I'm not interrupting your holidays, but I was wondering about your black vehicle, and where it was last night at approximately 11:45 in the evening?"

Out of those 26, I had mainly spoken to people with clear alibis, whose cars were safely parked in their garage while they hosted or attended some kind of festive gathering.

I knew it wasn't easy, but I had to keep going.

On call after call, I said the same monologue about needing to check the location of the registered black vehicles. I wrote those without alibi down for Wiggles to look into further.

It was all hands on deck and I was glad to have a job to do.

I just hoped Mrs Claus was okay; she had already broke down once today.

Fortunately, August was there with her. I was confident that there was no one more empathetic than my sister. She had always been caring, but had grown even more so since having baby Jeb. It must be her maternal side coming out. But whatever it was, it kept me at ease while I investigated away from Mrs Claus.

By the time I ended the 42nd call of the day, it was already past lunchtime, and my growling stomach made me realise that I hadn't eaten anything all day. If only Gilbert was here to remind me.

I had only known Gilbert for a few years and I was already lost without him. I couldn't imagine what it was like for Mrs Claus.

I stretched my back and finally stood up from my chair, just in time for Wiggles to return to his office. "I shouldn't keep you too long in here, Holly. Mrs Claus won't be pleased if she knows how hard I've had you working."

I shook my limbs to get the blood flow going after the hours of sitting still in a hunched-over position. "Well, I've just finished. I have some notes for you to look into."

"Just leave it on my table; I'll get back to it this afternoon. For now, I'd better drive you home."

"I'd appreciate that, but..."

"But...?"

"What about Gilbert? He has to be with us for Christmas dinner."

"We'll work around the clock until then," Wiggles assured me, holding the door open. "Come on, now. Let's get you home."

## 6

It took six and a half replays of *Last Christmas* on the stereo before we got back to Claus Cottage. By now, I knew that miles weren't the distance metric used when riding in Wiggles' Fiat; it was the number of times George Michael had to sing the same song.

If he was singing live, I felt sure that even he would have grown sick and tired of this song – but not Wiggles. And definitely not me, especially if it kept Wiggles happy. Yet, I had to admit, I was glad I didn't have to listen to this song for the rest of the day.

Upon seeing Father Christmas' sleigh parked up front, I almost jumped out of Wiggles' car. I was so anxious to know whether Father Christmas had managed to find the Yule Lads and, more importantly, Gilbert.

"Thank you, Wiggles! And Merry Christmas!" I shouted as I jogged up to the house as nimbly as I could, considering the white blanket of snow on the ground.

"Please let Gilbert be inside," I whispered to myself.

My gaze was fixated on the front door; I was so ready to walk in and find Gilbert complaining about Mrs Claus baking a hundred mince pies in *his* kitchen without his help. He'd get angry at August for making hot chocolates. He'd scold me for skipping meals. He'd threaten to hang his apron up and leave.

But as my boot hit the ground right at the front door, something red and green caught my eye. No, it wasn't the endless red and green decorations everywhere, it was... a person.

I felt my breath hitch as I gazed at the unmoving figure on the ground, a thin layer of snow delicately covering her body like a shroud. The pristine white contrasted sharply with her vibrant green work jumpsuit and the glint of her red cat-eye glasses. Snowflakes clung to her eyelashes, and her normally rosy cheeks were pale against the cold. It was Gwen. The sight of her, so still and vulnerable, sent a jolt of fear through me, making my heart pound in my chest. The serene, wintry scene around us felt eerie and unsettling.

The doctor in me quickly got into action, running towards unconscious Gwen, inspecting her for visible wounds, and checking her pulse.

Her lips were turning blue, and she was cold to the touch. Her pulse was weak. How long had she been lying on the cold ground?

Now that I was looking at it, I could see that the driveway up to Claus Cottage had been plowed of snow and even the garden decorations had been cleared from snow building up.

Gwen must've done it after we sent her on her way.

Oh, no.

I had to get her inside fast.

"Holly!" A voice echoed from a not-so-far distance, making me think that the panic was making me hear Santa's voice. But as I turned, Nick ran towards me.

"Nick," I called out, my breath coming out in a mist from the cold. "Help me get Gwen inside! We have to keep her warm."

Nick immediately swooped Gwen into his strong arms. Even in his Santa suit, you could see how sculpted his biceps were. But this was not the time to admire Nick.

Right.

Running into the house, Nick and I would've kicked the front door down if we had to, but without having to, we entered into utter chaos.

That's right – utter chaos.

There was no other definition for it. I counted eight, nine, and ten troll-like elves with pointed ears, huge noses, prominent facial hair, and short and long hair all gathered in the den. They shouted, jumped, and ran around the room while chowing down on cake, biscuits, and candies.

It was the Yule Lads!

The menacing little creatures who had been inconveniencing everyone's Christmas Eve with their pesky antics.

Since I had first entered Claus Cottage, I had never seen this place anywhere near as messy and loud. It was so messy and loud that no one even noticed Nick slip into the guest room with an unconscious elf in his arms, or me as I followed close behind him.

I could tell that even Nick was surprised by the uncultured guests, but he had bigger things to worry about, like keeping Gwen alive.

Nick carefully set Gwen on the bed, her body limp and cold to the touch. The soft, warm blankets seemed to engulf her, contrasting sharply with the chill that clung to her. Her green work jumpsuit was damp from the melting snow, and her skin had taken on a pallor that made her appear even more fragile. Nick gently adjusted her position, ensuring she was comfortable, his movements tender and precise. The room's warm glow from the bedside lamp highlighted the stark difference between the cozy, inviting space and Gwen's cold, vulnerable state.

"What do we do?" Nick asked out of pure concern.

"Gradually get her warm," I answered. It's an easy thing to get wrong because the temptation is to get a cold person as hot as possible as fast as possible. But that's dangerous. Instead, I put a single layer of blanket over Gwen, then cupped her cheeks with my hands after I rubbed them together for heat.

As Nick turned up the heater in the room one temperature higher every minute, I added another layer of blanket. Then another.

And another.

And another.

Until finally, the colours on Gwen's face began to return to normal.

Sighing in relief, Nick rubbed my back consolingly. "Now, we just have to wait for her to wake up. But first things first, who is she?"

"Her name's Gwen," I replied. "She's from Elf Employment. She came here earlier saying she was sent here as... Gilbert's replacement."

"So soon?"

"I know."

"And I reckon you kicked her out, and you kicked her so hard that she lost consciousness and collapsed in the snow?" Nick quipped; and as he smiled at me, the dimple in his cheek smiled at me too.

I tried to ignore his unconscious flirting as I laughed a little. "If you say it like that, I sound like a villain. But no, I promise I didn't kick her. We politely declined her services and sent her on her way."

"But she didn't leave?"

"It doesn't look like it. I just had the same thought when I saw her unconscious in the snow."

Nick nodded. "Elves can be stubborn. Alright, so that answers that. Now, to the second question, what's happening downstairs?"

"Oh, you mean the Yule Lads?"

"Those are the Yule Lads?"

I gawked at Nick in question. "I'm assuming they are. Wait, you haven't seen the Yule Lads before?"

"In books. But not in real life. It's funny, I had a dream about them when I was younger." Nick shrugged his shoulders.

Glancing at Gwen, whose breathing seemed better, I said to Nick. "We should probably help control the situation down there."

Taking my hand, Nick and I walked out of the guest bedroom only to get caught by Mrs Claus on our way out.

"Goodness gumdrops!" I exclaimed. Mrs Claus stood right outside the doorway.

Although it was small, Mrs Claus had a teasing smile on her face – the first smile I had seen her wear since last night. "Were you just alone in the guest bedroom?"

"It's not like that, Mum," Nick quickly turned Mrs Claus away, not wanting to make her worry more by seeing another elf in distress.

I immediately closed the door before Mrs Claus could glimpse Gwen on the bed.

As Nick led Mrs Claus back to the den, Mrs Claus abruptly stopped walking. "Nick, honey, aren't you supposed to be at the HQ? What are you doing here?

"I finished all my work early to help with Gilbert's search. I'll be back for the traditional sleigh ride tonight."

"But you shouldn't be here"

"Trust me, Mum. Mitzy has everything in order at HQ."

"But..." Mrs Claus hesitated, swallowing back her words. "Well, I suppose it's going to be fine. Come along."

I didn't think Nick noticed it, but Mrs Claus was definitely hiding a secret. She had the same expression Father Christmas had this morning after I asked them about Yule Lads kidnapping elves.

Something was up, but I didn't want to impose and ask what it was. So, I pursed my lips and followed Mrs Claus back to the rowdy den.

"Everyone!" Mrs Claus called for the Yule Lads' attention but failed.

Even Father Christmas bellowed. "Silence, please!"

Still, nothing.

So, Nick gave it a try. "Silence, everyone!"

Just like that, the room fell silent. Only the sound of a clattering utensil could be heard.

Perhaps it was the Santa suit that gave him such power over the mystical and menacing creatures.

"Oh, new Santa!" One of the giddy Yule Lads clapped.

However, the older Yule Lad, with silver hair and seemingly innocent sleepy eyes, spoke. "Is that little Nick Claus? You're so much bigger now. Much, much bigger –"

Father Christmas cleared his throat loudly. "If you will, gentlemen, please have a seat while we talk contract terms."

For a moment, no one moved, so Father Christmas added. "Or no peppermint bark for anyone."

Just like that, the Yule Lads politely sat right where they were – on the settee, on the floor, on the coffee table, under the Christmas tree, and even an inch too close to the burning furnace. Like trained puppies begging for treats.

"Thank you," Father Christmas rolled out a scroll on the coffee table after pushing the bitten pastries and used dishes to the side. "Now, I'd like all of you to sign our usual contract. A prank-free Candy Cane Hollow for ten years in exchange for exclusive use of the Frozen Flowering Forest."

There was a groan in the crowd.

Nick and I watched the negotiation happen from the corner of the room.

One after another, the Yule Lads had complaints and demands about the contract, saying it was outdated, overused, unnecessary, disrespectful, and whatever other adjectives popped into their minds. One of them even said it was bucolic, and I had the distinct impression he didn't know what the word meant.

Father Christmas initially shot down their objections, but eventually he realised that the Yule Lads weren't going to given in.

"How about we add a new clause? As a gesture of goodwill?"

"What kind of clause?" One of the Yule Lads paused from picking his nose to enquire. I tried not to shudder.

"Well, how about this. A monthly delivery of peppermint bark candies. How does that sound?"

The Yule Lads collectively groaned in satisfaction, and at least two began to salivate right there at the thought of their favourite treat being delivered to them so regularly.

The Yule Lads began signing on the contract's dotted lines. After they had all signed, Mrs Claus gave them goodie bags with peppermint bark candies.

After the last Yule Lad had collected his candies from Mrs Claus, Father Claus finally got to the most important thing. "Now that you've signed the contract, I need you to hand over Gilbert to us. This joke has been taken too far, and the poor elf might be afraid."

The Yule Lads exchanged curious and confused glances, muttering at one another.

"Elf?"

"Gilbert?"

"Who? What?"

Just as I was starting to think they didn't know anything, Father Christmas said. "You can't fool me, boys. Pathological lying is in your nature."

One of them snickered and said. "Sure, we have him…"

All ten of them laughed…as if Gilbert's disappearance was a laughing matter!

I took offence to their behaviour despite being warned that it was their nature. I stepped forward. "This is not a laughing matter. Gilbert is family to us. If you have him, please bring him home."

"There's an abundance of elves in this town. Just pick a new one!" Another one joked, sending his companions into another laughing fit.

I would've said more, but Mrs Claus touched my arm and shook her head with a soft expression. She moved to the middle of the room and spoke diplomatically. "Boys, just tell us honestly. Do you have Gilbert?"

With so many of them, it was hard to keep track of who was talking, but someone answered. "We don't have him. We don't need a fourteenth elf!"

I would've believed them if they didn't snicker, laugh, and hit each other playfully.

Judging by Mrs Claus' heavy sigh, it was apparent she knew talking to the Yule Lads was a hopeless cause, so she dismissed them. "Very well. I suggest you all run back to

No Carols Cave before I take your peppermint bark candies."

As if that was the most harrowing threat they could imagine, the Yule Lads grabbed their goodie bags and hurried out the front door.

Without the Yule Lads in the room, the silence was piercing. I broke it first. "So, that does it? No more pranks? That means they'll bring Gilbert back, right?"

"Not yet," Father Christmas carefully rolled the contract into a scroll. "All thirteen Yule Lads must sign for the contract to take effect. We still have to find the other three."

## 7

"We'll be back before dinner, I promise." Nick squeezed my hand consolingly as he prepared to step out with Father Christmas to find the remaining three Yule Lads.

For a moment, I held onto his hand, searching for reassurance. "With Gilbert, right?"

Nick hesitated. I knew he wouldn't want to make any promises he wasn't sure he could keep. So, he replied. "We'll try our best, Holly. For now, you should get some rest. I heard you went out early this morning to visit No Carols Cave, and you even helped Wiggles back at Candy Cane Custody."

"Well, I have to do something..." *Or I might lose my mind thinking about Gilbert*. This, I didn't say. I didn't want Nick to worry about me, too.

Nick kissed my hair, easing my anxieties momentarily. There was no gasp of pleasure from Mrs Claus, who loved to catch us embracing. She was too focused on Gilbert, as we all were. "You can take care of Gwen. And my mum. She may not say it straight to me, but I know she's worried sick. I mean, one hundred mince pies?"

Of course. Just like me, Mrs Claus wanted to keep herself occupied.

"It's because the Yule Lads had been stealing baked goods all morning," I explained.

"I heard. I couldn't be more thankful to you and August for helping her." Nick paused. "But those Yule Lads, I just want to say... they seem so familiar."

"You did grow up reading books and hearing all about them, so of course, they're familiar."

"No, it's different... they looked exactly like they did when I dreamed about them as a child."

"You have a good imagination," I said with a smile.

Over Nick's shoulders, I could see Father Christmas pull over outside with Dasher. He called out with this deep voice, full of authority, warmth and festivity. "Son, let's go!"

Nick turned for the door, smiling at me one last time. "I'll see you later."

I nodded, giving Father Christmas a small wave good-bye. "See you both tonight! Take care!"

As the sleigh sped out of sight, I closed the front door and found Mrs Claus smiling at me from the kitchen hall-way. "Don't worry too much, dear. The Yule Lads may be unruly, but they're not dangerous."

"That's a relief," I admitted. "I'm so scared for poor Gilbert."

Mrs Claus' smile slowly faded. "Tell me, were you able to find anything with Wiggles and Cornelius, dear?"

I walked closer to her. "We know Gilbert *voluntarily* got into a black vehicle before he disappeared."

"A black vehicle?"

"Yes, and so, we've spoken to almost all owners of registered black vehicles here in Candy Cane Hollow. But so far, that's all."

I could taste the bitter disappointment on the base of my tongue.

"No leads?" Mrs Claus held back a sigh.

"I'm sorry, Mrs Claus. I wish I had better news."

"And you're sure he voluntarily got into the car?"

I nodded as I replayed the footage in my mind. "He did look a little alarmed, but he opened the door and climbed in on his own."

"Well, let's just say I'm glad the situation's not getting worse."

The sweet cooing of my nephew Jeb came from behind us and I turned to see Tom holding the baby. I cocked my head to the side and smiled as I noted that they were wearing matching Christmas jumpers.

"Oh! Don't the two of you look adorable!" Mrs Claus gushed at the sight of them.

Tom grinned. "This monster won't let me put him down for a second. He's awful clingy. Teething, I guess. We blame everything on teething."

Mrs Claus laughed. "And if my memory serves me right, I'm sure it's usually the correct thing to blame."

"Shall I take him for a bit?" I offered.

Tom gave me a grateful smile. "I could do with popping to the little boys' room, if you're sure you don't mind?"

I held my arms out and focused on ignoring Mrs Claus' wistful gaze. I knew she was desperate to become a grandmother. Jeb was heavier and bigger every single time I held him, I was sure. He came to me happily and I rocked him in my arms.

"Why don't you take him in the den, dear? I'll make hot chocolates."

"That sounds lovely," I said. Tom remained in the kitchen doorway watching his son. "Go on, we're quite okay. And don't rush. I'll be happy to have some time with my nephew, won't I? Yes I will!"

I carried Jeb into the den where a quiet murmur of festive hymns was playing on the radio. I sat him on my knee on the floor and reached to the coffee table, where an old book of Christmas poems was. The pages were filled with old-fashioned illustrations of Christmas past and I found that the scenes were comforting.

"Ee!" Jeb squealed as one particular page caught his attention. He banged the page with his tiny hand and I laughed.

"Okay, Mr, you want this one?"

He nestled in to me and I cleared my throat, then began to read. "In Claus Cottage, where snowflakes gleam, A hidden treasure, like a dream. Behind the hearth where fires glow, Beneath the mistletoe's gentle show. Seek the star atop the tree, A clue lies there for all to see.

Follow the bells, hear their chime,"

"Find the treasure, it's Christmas time!" Mrs Claus joined in for the last line as she entered the room with a tray of hot chocolates for me and her and a small cup of warm milk for Jeb.

"You know this one?" I asked.

"Everyone knows that poem, dear. It's every child's favourite. Although it looks like Jeb is unimpressed!"

I glanced down and realised that Jeb had fallen to sleep in my arms. I leaned over and planted a gentle kiss on the top of his head. He was such a darling.

～

JUST THEN, I heard a thump from upstairs – from the guest bedroom, making Mrs Claus look up at the ceiling.

Biting my lip, I confessed to Mrs Claus. "Forgive me, Mrs Claus. Gwen is upstairs resting. But I guess she's awake now."

Mrs Claus' eyebrows furrowed together in thought. "Gwen is here? I thought you sent her on her way earlier."

"We did, but Nick and I found her a little while ago. She was outside, unconscious in the snow."

Mrs Claus' mouth opened in horror. "Oh no! Why didn't you tell me sooner? Was that why you and Nick were in the guest bedroom?"

Without waiting for my answer, Mrs Claus hurried up the stairs. I carefully rose from the carpet with Jeb in my arms and placed him in his crib, then followed Mrs Claus down the hallway towards the guest bedroom. "With the Yule Lads running around and all, I didn't want to give you something else to think about."

"Of course, dear. And don't get me wrong, that's really thoughtful of you. But we better check on her."

Mrs Claus didn't slow down until we got to the guest bedroom, where the door was open and a flurry of activity came from within.

Despite collapsing less than an hour ago, we caught Gwen folding all the blankets we had used to keep her warm.

"Oh my, sweet girl, stop folding those blankets this instant!" Mrs Claus stepped in, worried about Gwen's health. "You're still recovering."

Her face red with embarrassment, Gwen got in a tug of war with Mrs Claus over the duvet. "Please, no, Mrs Claus. My apologies for causing you such a humiliating inconvenience."

"Humiliating?" I echoed, gently pulling Gwen away from the duvet. "You passed out from the cold, Gwen. When we found you, you were blue and barely breathing!"

Gwen put a hand over her face, seemingly more embarrassed than alarmed. "Oh, I was just going to show you how efficient and hardworking I am as an elf by cleaning up all the snow outside! I never meant to cause you this bother."

Mrs Claus cooed, leading Gwen to the ottoman at the end of the bed where they both sat. "I appreciate your effort, Gwen, but why would you do something so reckless like that? You're not even dressed appropriately to be plowing snow!"

I could still see Gwen's eyes twinkling despite Mrs Claus scolding her. She answered. "After you sent me away despite my credentials, I couldn't just leave! Elf Employment sent *me* as one of the best elves in the business!"

"I bet you are one of the best; I don't doubt that. But you can only stay the best if you're feeling your best." Mrs Claus and her wise words resonated with me. I had given a similar speech to several patients over the years who were working themselves towards burnout in their careers. "You can't work if you're sick."

Gwen's face lit up, jumping on her seat. "You mean you're letting me work with you once I get better!?"

"No, no," Mrs Claus quickly cleared the air before things got lost in translation. "Calm down, Gwen, I'm not saying you can work here – I'm saying you can't work at all! Not in this condition. I suggest you rest up for now."

"But this cottage... Father Christmas, Nick, and you. Who will take care of all of you now Gilbert's gone?"

"He'll be back," Mrs Claus said with confidence. "You'd be surprised at how stubborn Gilbert is. He definitely won't leave without having the last word, I guarantee!"

"But it's a dereliction of his duties, Mrs Claus, to walk away! Perhaps I can work for you in the meantime. After all, it's Christmas Eve. You'll need a helping hand." Gwen remained optimistic.

Mrs Claus shook her head, glancing at me with kind eyes. "It wouldn't do. Gilbert is sensitive. He wouldn't want someone else to have helped, even for a short time."

Gwen gave a smile. "He wouldn't have to find out."

"I have all the help I could need right here in this home, Gwen. Please don't worry about me. I'll speak to Elf Employment and make sure they know our insistence is nothing against you."

"No!" Gwen exclaimed, causing me to jump. "Please don't speak to them. I'll explain everything myself."

Mrs Claus nodded her agreement. "Very well. But you're free to stay here until you feel better. Then, I'll arrange for someone to drive you home. The least that agency could have done is let you have a vehicle to ride across here in."

Gwen let out a deep sigh. For a second, I thought she was disappointed we weren't letting her fill in Gilbert's position, even temporarily. But then, she mumbled. "I don't even know where I'd go, that's the truth. I have no family."

Hearing those words, my heart suddenly ached. I found myself empathising with Gwen. So, I said to Mrs Claus. "Maybe Gwen could spend Christmas Eve with us."

Mrs Claus didn't even give it a second thought. "That sounds like a wonderful idea, Holly! You know, Gwen, Claus Cottage is always open for guests. You could definitely spend the rest of the day here!"

"Oh no, Mrs Claus, I wouldn't want to impose. How shameless of me to have slept in your bed and now act like a guest!" Gwen protested, seemingly repulsed by the thought of being just a guest.

"But I insist!" Mrs Claus said. "Unless you have some-where better to be?"

"Of course not, nowhere's better than Claus Cottage!"

"Then you should stay," Mrs Claus replied conclusively, finally standing up to make it clear she wouldn't accept any further argument. "I'll go make some soup for you."

"Oh, no!" Gwen quickly got up to her feet, but Mrs Claus turned back at her with a glare, effectively stopping her.

I chuckled and assured Gwen. "Just rest up. I'll come and fetch you once the soup is ready."

It was hard not to admire Mrs Claus for her unfaltering generosity and kindness. Her loyalty, too. Knowing she was waiting for Gilbert, even if it meant we'd have to do the chores by ourselves for now.

While I was by no means a neat freak, I would be happy to help keep Claus Cottage tidy until I could hear Gilbert scold me for trying to do my bit.

## 8

The whirring sound of the blender echoed in the kitchen, harmonising with the gentle hum of Christmas carols playing softly in the background. Mrs Claus expertly pureed the ingredients for the chestnut soup with bacon and chives, her hands moving with practiced ease. The rich aroma of roasted chestnuts mingled with the smoky scent of bacon, creating a mouthwatering fragrance that filled the cozy kitchen. The soup, a velvety concoction, bubbled gently on the stove, releasing waves of savoury steam that promised warmth and comfort in every spoonful. And whoever said chestnuts had to be roasting in a fire for Christmas? They could also be in a soup that smelled heavenly, bringing festive cheer to each simmering pot.

I was slightly embarrassed that I couldn't be more helpful in the kitchen. I simply watched Mrs Claus and August work on two open stoves, frying the bacon, melting the butter, and adding the carrot, celery, leek, and shallots.

In my defence, I did cut the carrots, and my poor

attempts made August laugh. She had always been the one more talented in the kitchen.

"This smells divine," I told Mrs Claus as I brought the soup-filled bowls to the dinner table – a job I could be trusted with.

Mrs Claus chuckled. "Thank you, dear. You can say my second best recipe is chestnut soup."

"I don't think I've tried this before," I commented.

"How could you? Gilbert goes berserk if I even so much as touch a ladle!" Mrs Claus laughed, but it was short, almost sad at the end, as she cleared her throat. "Well, I better fetch Gwen."

"I'm here!" Gwen squeaked as she rushed into the dining room. "I've been here all this time."

"Then, why didn't you come in?" Mrs Claus crossed her arms over her chest.

"I couldn't handle seeing you slaving away, Mrs Claus! I went into the den and wiped the dust from under the coffee table. I suggest you have a word with Gilbert about remembering that spot in future."

"Slaving away is a bit of an exaggeration, don't you think? I'm simply making soup! And I told you to simply rest, dear."

"I couldn't possibly rest while the great Mrs Claus cooks! My ancestors would turn in their graves if they knew."

Mrs Claus clicked her tongue and wiggled her finger. "We're not going to have this argument over a bowl of soup, Gwen. Now, come and join us."

Mrs Claus also turned to me and August. "You two, come on now. Let's not wait for my second-best recipe to get cold."

As we were instructed, August and I joined Mrs Claus. Seeing Gwen rock on her heels back and forth, I said to her. "You should seize this opportunity, Gwen. Mrs Claus hasn't cooked this chestnut soup in a long time! And yet, here you are being offered a bowl."

Judging by how Gwen's face went from adamant to intrigued, I finally understood that Gwen adored Mrs Claus – as most elves did in Candy Cane Hollow.

There was no person, elf, or creature who wasn't completely smitten with Mrs Claus. The closest comparison I could come to was the way so many of my fellow British people had idolised the Queen. She was a calm, unflappable leader, even during hard times.

Glancing at the engagement ring on my finger, I felt slightly worried I might never come close to Mrs Claus' well-loved legacy.

I shook the thoughts away, knowing I had more important things to worry about.

I brought a spoonful of chestnut soup to my lips, the steam rising in delicate wisps. As the warm, velvety liquid touched my tongue, my taste buds immediately tingled with delight. Mrs Claus' soup deserved the second spot on her list of best recipes. The chestnut soup was a symphony of flavours—rich and buttery with a hint of smokiness from the bacon. The earthy chestnuts melded perfectly with the salty, savoury chives, creating a harmonious balance that was both comforting and indulgent. Each mouthful was a burst of festive warmth, enveloping my senses in holiday cheer.

Gwen also took her first spoonful and savoured it before saying. "Is that nutmeg I'm tasting?"

Mrs Claus grinned. "Well, well. Looks like someone knows her spices."

"Of course," Gwen blushed, putting down her spoon momentarily to produce a small notebook from her pocket.

"I have to write this down so I won't forget it. I hope that's alright."

"Go ahead. I'm flattered that you like my soup."

"I do! Not that my opinion matters to a Claus!" Gwen cheered as she furiously wrote in her notebook. After she was done, she put it back into her pocket. "Now that I'm having this tasty meal as a *guest,* I feel obliged to do something for you, Mrs Claus."

"You are a sly one," Mrs Claus teased. "Guests in Claus Cottage don't do anything for me or for anyone else!"

"But there must be something I could do," Gwen insisted between spoonfuls of soup. "It doesn't have to be a chore... something simple... something to show my appreciation... for this food!"

Gwen was one noisy eater, but no one at the table really minded. Mrs Claus seemed delighted that Gwen was enjoying her soup so much.

Shaking her head with a smile, Mrs Claus said. "Maybe we could think of something a guest could do."

August presented. "Oh! Maybe Gwen could come join Tom, Jeb, and me in delivering the mince pies."

I glanced at her. "You're delivering the mince pies?"

"Yep! I asked Mrs Claus to let me. It'll be a great way for me and my family to go around Candy Cane Hollow. I still haven't memorised all of the roads!"

"And Tom is alright with it?"

"Definitely. Jeb has been fussy all day – nothing a car ride can't fix, I promise."

I was tempted to go with August just so I had something to do, but I didn't want to leave Mrs Claus alone in the confines of Claus Cottage. Not when every corner of this place reminded us so much of Gilbert.

Mrs Claus responded. "I think that's a great idea. If

Gwen is up to it, I suppose she could join you. How about that, Gwen?"

"I'll do it! It's better than doing nothing, especially now that I've had my fill of soup!"

I laughed, not realising Gwen had already finished her bowl. "You really enjoyed it, huh?"

"Every last bit of it!" Gwen proudly said. Beside her, her mobile phone buzzed. Before she could pick it up, I had instinctively glanced at the screen and saw that it was Elf Employment ringing. Gwen glanced at the screen, gave a small tut, and refused the call.

"Take that call if you need to, dear," Mrs Claus said.

"Oh. No! It's bad manners! I'll call them back."

"Okay then. Well, we still have some soup left on the stove. Do you want a second serving?" Mrs Claus asked.

"I couldn't," Gwen said, although her face lit up at the possibility.

I laughed and shook my head. "I'll fetch it."

Gwen happily finished her second serving of soup once I placed it in front of her. That was no surprise, I couldn't imagine many people being able to resist such a tasty meal.

After eating, Gwen offered to do the dishes, but of course Mrs Claus didn't let her get near the sink. Was it really because Mrs Claus didn't want Gwen to do any chores, or was it because she was protective over Gilbert's space?

I didn't ask. Instead, I helped Mrs Claus clear the table and wash the dishes while Gwen went with August and her family to deliver the hundred mince pies.

The house was silent, with just Mrs Claus and me.

Before Gilbert disappeared, this house was never really empty – we'd always find Gilbert cleaning some corner or cooking something. And his dramatic personality meant that the house was rarely silent.

For a moment, we left the stillness of the house to its own quiet devices. Neither of us spoke as we finished the dishes.

With only two bowls left in the sink, Mrs Claus held one under the tap, the stream of water cascading over the ceramic surface, creating a soothing, rhythmic sound. The kitchen was filled with the lingering aroma of chestnut soup, and the soft glow of Christmas lights reflected off the wet dishes. Suddenly, the bowl slipped from her hands, the soapy surface betraying her grip. Time seemed to slow as the bowl fell, spinning slightly before crashing onto the other dirty bowl below. The sharp sound of breaking ceramic echoed through the room as the bowl shattered, sending fragments scattering and chipping the other bowl in the process.

"Mrs Claus!" I exclaimed, immediately slipping beside her to check her hands and fingers. "Are you alright?"

Mrs Claus' hand shook a little, but apart from that, she was okay.

"I'm so sorry, dear," Mrs Claus pulled her hand away and took a deep breath to calm herself. "This isn't like me. How embarrassing."

She turned to pick up the broken porcelain, but I stopped her. "I'll do it, Mrs Claus. I'll finish up in here."

Usually, Mrs Claus would argue just like she had with Gwen, but perhaps we had reached a point in the day where she couldn't bring herself to argue any longer.

Graceful as ever, Mrs Claus strode towards the nearby stool and sat herself down. "I don't ever break dishes, dear. Look at me, a few hours without Gilbert and I'm falling to pieces."

It was certainly right that I'd never seen Mrs Claus in

such a state in all my time in Candy Cane Hollow, so I nodded. "He'll be okay, Mrs Claus."

As I carefully picked up the large chunks of broken porcelain, Mrs Claus could no longer contain her thoughts. "I keep thinking about him – those thoughts keep nagging me."

I set aside the broken bowl and turned to face Mrs Claus, whose gaze fell directly in the distance beyond the window. Outside, the snow continued to fall. "I'm sure he's fine. The Yule Lads probably just hid him somewhere, but they won't hurt him. Right...?"

"I suppose not."

"And you'd know that best, Mrs Claus, because you told me they did something like this before, and I'm assuming no one got hurt."

"That's true, but –" Mrs Claus stopped herself.

I could tell she was debating whether to say whatever it was to me. Then, she patted the stool next to her. "Come here, dear. I suppose you have to know."

Curious, I wiped my hands and sat beside Mrs Claus. "What is it?"

"It's about Nick," she sighed. "It was roughly three decades ago when Nick was... kidnapped by the Yule Lads, just for fun. But it wasn't fun for us as his parents. That was how the contract came to be."

I gasped.

Now it made sense – why Father Christmas and Mrs Claus didn't want to talk about the other kidnapping and why Nick thought the Yule Lads were familiar.

"Does Nick know?" I asked.

"I don't think so, no. He was too young to have remembered anything. But when he disappeared... you can just imagine the panic. It's why my husband is so insistent on getting the contract in place again. Who knows what Gilbert is feeling right now?"

It was safe to say that nothing bad happened to Nick, but I still wondered what the Yule Lads had done while they had him. "Why did they take Nick?"

"They simply said the traditional stealing of pans and baked goods was getting boring, so they tried to stir things up by kidnapping a young boy just to play with him in the Frozen Flowering Forest."

"And they chose Nick?"

"Well, they didn't know he was Nick *Claus,* if that's what you're wondering."

"So, nothing bad happened?"

Mrs Claus shook her head. "Nothing bad happened to Nick, but his father and I? We almost turned Candy Cane Hollow upside down!"

I wasn't sure what to do with this information.

Playing with a bunch of elves in the scenic Frozen Flowering Forest didn't seem traumatic, and Nick couldn't even remember it. Still, it made Mrs Claus and Father Christmas' anxiety more real.

They had been here before and didn't want to be here again.

"So, what should we do, Mrs Claus?"

"There's only one thing we can do. Sit tight and wait for all the Yule Lads to sign the contract. Then, they'll have no choice but to end all their pranks, including hiding Gilbert."

## 9

M rs Claus and I had been staring out of the window overlooking the driveway for what felt like *hours*. We had refilled our mugs with hot chocolate twice now, even though every sip was a reminder that we were missing Gilbert.

After our conversation, all we could really do was wait. But being so helpless didn't feel good, and I was still thinking of ways to help with Gilbert's search. I had to trust that Father Christmas knew best, however. The Yule Lads had Gilbert, and they would give him back once the new contract was signed.

Our thoughts were interrupted by a sharp rap at the door. Again, part of me expected to hear Gilbert dash to ensure he was first to answer it, but of course no such sound came.

"I'll get it," I said. Mrs Claus didn't even seem to have heard the interruption.

I pulled open the door to see Ethan Evergreen on the doorstep. He gave me a grim smile.

"Ethan. What a surprise. Would you like to come in?" I asked. While I was sure that neither myself or Mrs Claus felt like company, we still had to act with courtesy towards people.

I led Ethan into the den, where he sat closest to the fire and held his hands out towards the flames for warmth.

"Shall I get you a drink?" I offered.

Ethan shook his head. "Please, allow me."

"Absolutely not, dear," Mrs Claus said. "Both Holly and I are capable of making drinks. Now, what would you like?"

"I won't trouble you for a drink, Mrs Claus. I only called in to see if there's any news on Gilbert."

I cocked my head a little and looked at Ethan more closely. His clothes were good-quality but old, at least a few seasons out of date. His shoes were in less than ideal condition, considering the weather. And he seemed colder than the short walk from town would have caused. It was clear that he had fallen on hard times, and yet he had been the person most concerned for Gilbert, outside of his family and the police.

"You're truly a good friend, Ethan," I said.

The man's cheeks flushed and he batted away the compliment as his eyes filled with tears. "No, I've been nowhere near good enough to Gilbert. That's the truth. I've been so distracted from what really matters."

"You're under a terrible strain, dear," Mrs Claus sympathised.

"I'll never forgive myself if something happens to him," Ethan said as he wiped his eyes.

"We're all staying positive. The police are working non-stop to identify Gilbert's kidnapper. They'll work out who made the call and make an arrest in no time. Just you watch," I said, with much more enthusiasm and belief than I actually felt.

Ethan's skin paled and he met my gaze. "But what if... what if someone hurts him?"

"Nonsense," Mrs Claus said, her voice hard and firm. "Nobody would dare hurt a Claus family house-elf."

Ethan nodded and rose from his chair. "I've taken enough of your time, ladies. May I visit the bathroom on my way out?"

"Of course, I'll -"

"No. I know where it is. I don't wish to trouble you any further," Ethan insisted, and he left the room.

I glanced at Mrs Claus, but she was busy gazing into the flames in the fireplace. They were hypnotic and seemed to be captivating her full attention. I decided not to disturb her.

A minute or two later Ethan poked his head in the doorway and said he would be on his way.

I showed him out and closed the door behind him, only then realising that he had failed to flush the toilet after him. His mind really must be all over the place.

I returned to the den and Mrs Claus and I continued to sit in silence, lost in our thoughts. After an agonising wait, at the end of the driveway, Father Christmas' sleigh rode up towards the cottage with Nick and three Yule Lads!

"Finally!" I breathed, making Mrs Claus look up.

She took a sharp intake of breath and said, "I'll get some peppermint bark."

I quickly ran to the front door, opening it just as Nick hopped down from the sleigh. His cheeks were flushed from the cold, but what was more glaring was the concerned look on his face as he carried one of the Yule Lads out of the sleigh.

The small Yule Lad winced, his face contorted in pain as he cradled his leg, his tattered clothes smeared with dirt and snow. His small, pointed ears twitched slightly, and his eyes were wide with distress.

"What happened?" I exclaimed, rushing out to meet Nick and the injured Yule Lad. The cold air bit at my cheeks, and the crunch of snow underfoot marked my hurried steps. Behind them were two other Yule Lads—one with a unibrow and a scowl etched deeply on his face, his arms crossed defensively. The other had a mischievous glint in his eye, glancing around nervously as if expecting trouble at any moment. The scene was a chaotic mix of worry and tension, the normally playful Yule Lads now overshadowed by an air of urgency and concern.

Father Christmas trailed behind them after petting Dasher for a job well done and giving the animal a carrot as reward.

"Slammer here tried to outrun us and fell off a roof in trying to do so," Nick explained.

Slammer? The Yule Lad who stomped on roofs and slammed doors?

"Let me look at him," I offered, feeling grateful to finally have a job I could do.

Nick nodded, heading inside with Slammer in his arms and then setting him down carefully on the settee in the den.

"Goodness gumdrops!" Mrs Claus jumped as she entered the den and placed the bowl of peppermint bark candies on the coffee table. "What happened?"

"Slammer here fell off a roof," Nick said.

Slammer glared at him. "I wouldn't have fallen if you didn't scare me!"

"I scared you?" Nick replied. "You immediately bolted when you saw us!"

"And you started chasing me!"

"I politely asked you, from a distance, to come down from the roof so we could talk!"

"Same difference!" Slammer whined. He sounded like a petulant child.

"Enough! Let me treat your injury before anything else," I instructed as I bent down to check Slammer's ankle.

The scowling Yule Lad stood next to me. "And who do you think you are to treat my brother?"

Father Christmas spoke. "She's a doctor, Scraper. Holly runs a clinic here in Candy Cane Hollow, and she's my future daughter-in-law. Now, have some peppermint bark candy and settle down."

Although I blushed at hearing Father Christmas refer to me as his future daughter-in-law, I had to focus more on Slammer's swollen ankle. "Did you hear a pop when you hit the ground? I'm assuming you've got a sprained ankle."

Slammer winced as I gently touched his leg. "I heard all sorts of things when I was falling. I even thought I heard my father from the grave!"

"So, you heard a pop?"

"That and other things!"

"Does it feel loose?"

"So loose I couldn't even put weight on it if I wanted to!"

"That does sound like a sprain," I concluded. "I'll go get some bandages. I'll have to apply compression on your ankle to reduce swelling, alright? I'll also get some pain medicine. You'll need it."

"I don't like the taste of medicines!" Slammer complained like a child who was about to get the flu shot he was so sure he didn't need.

Fortunately, I had plenty of experience getting reluctant children to take foul-tasting medicine. I tried negotiating with Slammer like I would with a child. "I'll give you a lollipop if you take it?"

"Well, I guess I could try..."

I chuckled as I exited the room to get bandages, pain medicine, and an ice pack.

By the time I returned to the den, the negotiations on the contract with the Yule Lads had begun.

Father Christmas was reading out the new clause. "... monthly deliveries and a lifetime supply of Peppermint Bark Candy, delivered directly to No Carols Cave."

Slammer remarked with multiple nods. "That sounds reasonable."

While Slammer and the other Yule Lad seemed convinced easily, Scraper shook his head. "A candy!? In exchange for stopping us doing the very things we were born to do? If you ask me, we're at a disadvantage here!"

From my periphery, I could see Father Christmas place the scroll contract before Scraper, pointing to the bottom part. "All ten other Yule Lads have already signed. No one thought it was anything but fair."

"That's because they're not thinking clearly!" Scraper slapped the other Yule Lad's hand as it reached for another candy. "You're bribing them with candies and clouding their judgment – that's why!"

I began wrapping the bandage around Slammer's ankle; he winced as I did so. But the sight of a big lollipop right on top of the first aid kit stopped Slammer from complaining too much.

Mrs Claus spoke. "Candies were the only way to get them to settle down. Yule Lads and candies go hand-in-hand like Rudolph and his red nose. It's a known fact!"

"But it does not apply to me," Scraper answered with pride. "Adding candies to a contract... ridiculous!"

I could feel Scraper's glare at the back of my head as I finished wrapping the bandage. He said. "Are you done there? I would like to leave with my brothers now."

"No one's leaving yet," Father Christmas argued. "Not until we finalise this contract for the next ten years."

"Well, I'm not signing it." Scraper insisted.

The Yule Lad beside him tugged the end of his coat. "Scraper... it's not that bad of a deal. We could definitely use some candy back at home."

"Climb a jelly bean tree or visit the Marshmallow Marsh, then. We don't need candies delivered to us! It's a mockery of who we are."

Nick, who had been standing in the corner of the room, stepped forward. "What do you mean by that? How do candies mock you?"

The other Yule Lad said. "Scraper has been on an all-protein diet for months now. That must be it."

So, Nick responded. "Then, would you like meat deliveries added to the contract as well?"

"What? No!" Scraper bellowed.

"Chocolate almonds?" Mrs Claus proposed.

"Twinkies, too!" Slammer added.

"So, more sweets?" Father Christmas asked the group, raising his pen to scribble in the contract if needed.

Then, Scraper snapped, jumping out of his seat. "This is not about sweets and candies! It's about how this contract has made us lose our purpose as Yule Lads! We're meant to play tricks, it's what we were born for."

With heaving breaths, Scraper continued – rather, he couldn't stop himself. "For generations, even before the Frozen Flowering Forest became frozen, Yule Lads were brought to this earth to play tricks! Our pranks used to be part of Christmas itself! But if we can't play tricks and pull pranks, our lives become pointless!"

Scraper glared at all of us, most especially at Father Christmas. "You think we enjoyed the last ten, twenty, and thirty years of looking forward to... nothing? Years and years of pointless living, but gathering logs for fire, fetching water from rivers and streams, and hunting food? You think that's what we were made for?"

I tried not to panic. Scraper was seriously unhappy. If he had kidnapped Gilbert in such a heightened state, I couldn't bare to imagine what may have happened to him.

Father Christmas was too stunned to speak. It was probably the first time that a Yule Lad – or any elf at that – had stood up against him.

As I put away my First Aid kit, I couldn't stop myself from replying. "Kidnapping people and elves are not just tricks and pranks."

"You're all still going on about that?" Scraper fired back. "It happened thirty years ago, and we didn't even know we took little Nick Claus! We were going to return him before dusk, anyway!"

My head immediately whipped in Nick's direction. His eyes were wide in surprise. "I was... kidnapped?"

Mrs Claus opened her mouth and closed it again.

From tending to Slammer, I stood up and touched Nick's arm. "You were. By the Yule Lads. So, it wasn't just a dream you had."

"You knew?" He turned to me and my heart clenched at the slight betrayal in his eyes.

"I just told Holly today," Mrs Claus chimed in, touching Nick's cheek lovingly. "We didn't tell you because nothing really happened. The Yule Lads were just playing with you, but it worried me and your father."

"To the point that your mother got sick," Father Christmas added.

"Well..." Mrs Claus shrugged her shoulder, neither confirming nor denying it.

Nick took his mother's hand and squeezed it. "I'm sorry that happened to you, Mum."

"It's alright, dear," Mrs Claus put her hand on top of Nick's. "I'm just glad nothing happened to you back then."

It was an emotional moment, until Scraper interrupted once more. "Exactly! Nothing happened! So, why have we been punished for decades!?"

Father Christmas sighed. "Slammer, Peeper, do you also feel this way? Like I have robbed you of your life's purpose?"

Peeper avoided Scraper's taunting gaze as he answered. "Well, it gets boring at the cave sometimes, but I don't mind not pranking anyone..."

Scraper's disapproval was evident.

"And Slammer?" Father Christmas turned to the injured Yule Lad, who was licking his lollipop after popping a pain pill.

"To be honest, stomping on roofs and slamming doors is not as entertaining as it sounds," Slammer replied.

"Foolish! Both of you!" Scraper yelled, marching towards the door with a final remark. "I'm not signing that contract! That'll be the death of me! No wonder your elf left! It must be because of how intolerable the Clauses are!"

My ears rang at Scraper's final remarks.

He headed straight for the door, Peeper running after him with a handful of candies and Slammer limping along behind with his new crutch.

"Thanks, doctor!" Slammer shouted on his way out.

Father Christmas looked at the unsigned scroll, defeated. Then, Mrs Claus suddenly plopped down on the nearby chair as if she had lost her footing.

"Mum!" Nick swiftly ran to her side.

"Is that true?" Mrs Claus' voice was melancholic. "Did Gilbert leave because we're...intolerable?"

## 10

The little daisy-like flowers bobbed gently on the surface of the golden liquid inside the clear teacup as I carefully carried it to Mrs Claus' bedroom. The warm, fragrant aroma of chamomile wafted up, mingling with the faint scent of vanilla that filled the air. The cup's delicate glass glinted softly in the light, casting tiny reflections on the wooden floor as I walked. The soothing sight of the flowers floating serenely atop the tea promised a moment of peace and comfort amidst the day's turmoil. Or at least, I hoped they would.

I found Nick standing in the hallway outside his parents' bedroom.

"It's chamomile tea with honey," I explained. "This will help her calm down."

"Alright," Nick, like the gentleman that he was, turned the doorknob open for me but paused before he opened the door. "Can we talk after you bring that to Mum?"

I stared at him, seeing nothing but worry etched on his face. So, I nodded. "Definitely. I'll be right back."

Nick pushed the door open, letting me into the

bedroom, where I found Mrs Claus lying on the bed while Father Christmas massaged her hand. It was a heart-warming scene, but Mrs Claus groaned with sadness.

"I brought some chamomile tea," I called out from the other end of the room, carefully bringing it to the bedside table.

"Thank you," Father Christmas said. "Don't worry too much about Mrs Claus; she often gets feverish when she's stressed."

"Psychogenic fever," I mumbled through force of habit, pointing to the edge of the bed. "May I?"

Father Christmas nodded.

I sat down on the edge of the bed, the mattress shifting at my weight. Mrs Claus opened her eyes to look at me.

I said. "You know what Scraper said isn't true, right? Gilbert would never leave Claus Cottage. He would never leave his *home*."

Mrs Claus looked away and into a bare space on the wall. "I don't know anymore. It's been sixteen hours since Gilbert disappeared. And the Yule Lads, oh, they're a dead end."

"If they intended to return Nick before, maybe they're also planning on doing the same thing to Gilbert." I tried to be logical, maybe hopeful.

"Nick wasn't gone for sixteen hours,"

"Well, maybe they're waiting until Christmas."

"I don't know," Mrs Claus turned to her side on the bed, her back facing me.

Truly, Mrs Claus had been high on her emotions for hours on end; she must be utterly drained.

Father Christmas offered me a small smile. "Let's let her rest for now. She'll be up and running again before we know it."

I nodded. "Of course. Let me know if there's anything else I can do."

I left the room, a sharp, aching pain gripping my chest, as if my heart had been wrenched from my ribs. Each step felt heavy, burdened by the sight of Mrs Claus in such a state. My emotions churned, a tumultuous mix of sorrow and helplessness that defied description. The memory of her tear-streaked face and trembling hands haunted me, stirring feelings that were far from comforting. The weight of her grief settled deep within me, an inescapable reminder of the anguish we all shared.

Closing the bedroom door behind me, Nick anxiously paced in the hallway.

"Hey..." I touched his back, making him pause from all the pacing.

"I can't stand seeing Mum like this. We need to find Gilbert," Nick told me with urgency. "Dad told me you came with them to No Carols Cave, so you must know the way, right?"

"I do, but I'm sure Father Christmas also told you that Gilbert wasn't in their cave."

"Yes, but the Frozen Flowering Forest is vast. Maybe he's being held somewhere else. We have to find him."

"I know," I took both of Nick's hands, cold and sweaty. "But you have to calm down first. Mrs Claus is fine – she will be fine. But if she sees you like this, she might worry more. So, let's talk this through. Do you have a plan for finding Gilbert?"

Frustrated, Nick ran a hand on his face. "No! I don't. I just know I have to bring Gilbert home."

"Okay, well, we can come up with a plan. But first, I'll give Wiggles a call and see if there are any developments on the search."

"Alright, let's do that."

I walked Nick away from his parents' bedroom so Mrs Claus wouldn't hear our conversation.

As soon as we were out of earshot, I dialled Wiggles' number on my phone. He immediately picked up. "Hello?"

"Wiggles, it's Holly... again," I said with a chuckle. "I'm just calling to check up on Gilbert's case. Is there any development? Any new leads?"

"Cornelius and I just visited some of the people on our list with the black vehicles, but so far, we haven't found anything that could point us to Gilbert."

"Right... how about any tips? Any clues at all?"

"Holly, you'll be the first person I call if we find anything."

I felt bad for pestering Wiggles, but Nick was watching me with anticipation. "You don't mind if I also look for Gilbert, right? With Mrs Claus' blessing, of course!"

After a few seconds, I could hear *Last Christmas* playing in the background down the phone, indicating he was in his car now. "I did hear that your sister delivered mince pies to Candy Cane Custody. I hope Mrs Claus isn't mad I borrowed you for a while?"

"Not at all," I assured him. "So, I'll start my own independent investigation. Is that all right?"

"Sure, sure. We'll keep driving around town and see what useful information we can find." Wiggles replied.

"I'll also give you a call if I find anything."

The line clicked as the call ended.

"So?" Nick immediately said.

I shook my head apologetically. "They haven't found any new leads yet."

"Okay, that's alright. We can just come up with our own plan." Nick seemed to be convincing himself more than me.

Seeing how Gilbert's disappearance was getting under everyone's skin, I knew Nick was right—we had to find Gilbert. Soon.

Right there and then, I racked my brain for a plan.

At that moment, I knew we needed other people's help if we wanted to find Gilbert before Christmas dinner. So, I said. "We need reinforcements. If more people are looking, we'll find Gilbert faster."

"Okay, that's a good start." Nick faltered. "But it's Christmas Eve. Who would even want to help us right now?"

"People who care about us, about Gilbert." I paused to think. "Like...his cousin Patrice!"

"Oh, and Ginger! She used to say she'd love to put Gilbert in a bag and take him home!"

"Now we're talking. I'll go call Patrice and tell her to meet us at the Polar Arms."

WITH THE SLIPPERY ROADS, Nick and I brought a sleigh to the Polar Arms, the cozy pub where Ginger Rumples, Nick's childhood best friend, worked. The pub was one of my favourite places in Candy Cane Hollow, with its roaring fire, comfortable chairs and extensive board game collection. The walls were plastered with advertisements for upcoming community events, and an especially garish poster caught my eye. It promised 50% off everything at Evergreen Emporium.

"What in Candy Cane Hollow is that?" I asked Ginger with a smile as she placed two cocktail glasses before us, each filled with red liquid.

Ginger, an experienced bartender, would earn extra

points for the drink presentations if we were scoring her. The glasses were elegantly rimmed with a festive mix of red and white sprinkles, adding a delightful crunch with each sip. A striped candy cane served as a whimsical stirrer, infusing a subtle minty sweetness into the beverages. The vibrant colours and playful garnish made each drink look like a miniature holiday celebration, enticing both the eyes and the palate.

"I call it Santa's Sleigh Ride," Ginger snorted at how ridiculous the name sounded. "It's a working title. Don't judge me."

As I admired the glass, Nick said. "I don't think we should be drinking right now, Ginger."

Ginger threw a dismissive hand at Nick's direction. "Oh, come on. Do you really think I'd try and get you drunk at such an important time? It's a mocktail, Nick."

"Oh," Nick chuckled. "Well, thank you."

After Ginger set aside the glasses in front of her, she leaned over from behind the bar. "So, I heard Gilbert's missing."

"That's actually why we're here," Nick began. "We need your help. It's been sixteen, seventeen hours since Gilbert disappeared."

Ginger nodded understandingly. "They say the first twenty-four hours are the most important. I heard that on some true crime show."

I winced at the suggestion that Gilbert was in a true crime show kind of situation.

"Will you help us?" Nick asked.

Ginger's long auburn plait bobbed as she nodded enthusiastically. "But how do you think I can help? I'm sure Holly's the better detective between the two of us."

"We can't really investigate on the few clues we have," I

admitted.

"You know a lot of people and elves in town – their contact numbers and addresses," Nick added. "We figured there's no better person who could help us call or visit as many homes as we can in Candy Cane Hollow."

If Ginger wasn't courteous, she would've dropped her jaw wide open at us. But instead, she just blinked. "You want to call or visit *all* the homes in town?"

"We're a little desperate," Nick confessed with slight shame. He was the new Santa-in-training after all; he ought to do more for Gilbert, but he couldn't.

"Okay, well, you know what, I'm just happy to help. Let me grab my coat." Ginger said, making her way into the door behind her with the sign 'Employees Only.'

As she disappeared into the other room, I checked my phone to see if Patrice was on her way. She had agreed to meet us at the pub.

As I debated sending a message checking how long she would be, Patrice dashed in through the front door of the Polar Arms; the sleigh that dropped her off was decorated in ornate gold patterns.

Was it actual gold? Maybe. Patrice had the money for it.

"I'm so sorry it took me a while!" Patrice fussed as she ran towards the bar with some paper bags in her arms. It was clear that she had been crying and her voice sounded wobbly enough that I didn't trust her not to start again.

Patrice was dressed impeccably, flaunting her newfound fortune with an elegant green coat that shimmered subtly under the lights, the fabric rich and luxurious. A plush red scarf, lined with soft, fluffy faux fur, draped stylishly around her neck, adding a festive touch to her ensemble. The scarf's fur caught the light, creating a warm halo effect that complemented her vibrant attire. Her overall appearance was one of sophistication and opulence, exuding a confidence that matched her newly acquired wealth.

Nick helped her up onto a bar stool, and she muttered her thanks. "I was in the middle of buying Christmas gifts for you all; I didn't think I would see any of you until after the holidays. Here..."

Patrice slid the paper bags toward us.

"Patrice, you didn't have to," I said.

"After everything you all did for me, of course I had to!" Patrice insisted.

Nick set aside the paper bags for now. "Thanks, Patrice. Most especially, thank you for coming to meet us on Christmas Eve."

"I can't believe Gilbert's missing. He's always been so... so... dependable! I have a feeling something awful must have happened to him!" Patrice exclaimed, and sure enough, she began to cry again.

"And that's why we need your help," I discussed. "We figured you may have some resources to spare to find Gilbert."

Patrice listened in between big, gulping sobs. "What do you need me to do?"

I glanced at Nick, who explained our plan. "Well, we have Wiggles and Cornelius roving the streets, and Ginger's going to help us check other people's properties in case the Yule Lads have the cheek to hide Gilbert right here in Candy Cane Hollow!"

"They wouldn't dare, surely!" Patrice asked.

"At this point, we just don't know," I explained.

"I can help go door to door," Patrice offered.

Nick shook his head. "We need someone to help us search the Frozen Flowering Forest as quickly as possible."

"Frozen Flowering Forest?" Patrice wiggled her nose. "But isn't that the forest no one could find?"

"Well, my dad told me that only Clauses can pierce the veil hiding it – so, I'm coming with you. Holly knows the way."

"Alright. I can think of one way we could scout an entire forest quickly." Patrice replied.

"How?" I asked.

"Drones," Patrice confidently answered. "And I happen to have about fifty high-quality drones we could send out in any weather, at any altitude."

Slight relief washed over me. Despite the uncertainty of where our search would lead us, things were finally looking up.

As I turned to Nick, he gave me a soft smile. "Let's do it."

"I'm here!" August arrived outside the Polar Arms wearing a beanie, a scarf, and gloves. She was having a hard time adjusting to the much colder climate of Candy Cane Hollow. I mean, we're British, it's not as if we're used to tropical temperatures, but our usual weather tolerance was around the *grey and drizzly* level, not the constant chill and snow of this winter wonderland. "What did you say we're doing again?"

"You're coming with me," Ginger snaked her arm around August's arm, friendly as ever. Those two had bonded really well, which was a surprise to me. Ginger was so fiery and fun, and August was so domestic and mild. "We have about... ninety-six homes to visit all before Christmas dinner."

"Ninety-six!?" August exclaimed, looking at me for help.

"Sorry, sis," I smiled. "We need everyone to look for Gilbert."

"Don't worry, Wiggles and Cornelius are also checking out some houses. I also have some of my friends checking their own neighbourhoods, so we're actually down to twenty-two. I can be efficient, right?" Ginger said.

"Oh," I could see the relief in August's face. "Twenty-two isn't so bad. You should've started with that."

"I like surprising people," Ginger remarked with a wink, as she led August by the arm towards her Mini Cooper. "Come on, let's do it, you child of the summer!"

Yep, as her name suggested, August was born in, well, August. The height of summer in Britain, but don't be misled by that. It was still mainly a grey and drizzly month most years.

I turned to Nick, who was already waiting in front of his sleigh. Behind him was Patrice, and in the back compartment were several high-tech drones waiting to do their thing.

As I climbed up and sat next to Patrice, I felt a bit more hopeful. We had Wiggles and Cornelius on the streets, August and Ginger plus several of her friends on the door to door search, and then Nick, Patrice, and me off to the Frozen Flowering Forest.

While assuming that Gilbert wasn't hidden well was a gamble, hopefully we'd at least find clues about where the Yule Lads had hidden him.

However impossible it seemed, I just knew we had to try.

I instructed Nick on the directions leading to the Frozen Flowering Forest. It wasn't that hard to do until all the landmarks turned to vast lands of nothing but white snow, and the streets and pathways turned to... more snow.

There was a moment when I was starting to think we were lost, but as we navigated the blinding snow, a thick mist – much like a cloud – caught my attention.

"That way!" I pointed at Nick.

Nick looked sceptical as he led the sleigh in that direction. After all, the mist was so thick that you couldn't see what was on the other side. If it were a cliff, we'd just plummet to our deaths. That is, of course, if we weren't riding in a sleigh pulled by flying reindeer. It was easy to forget that sometimes and imagine we were trotting along on some sky highway.

After several seconds of flying through the thick fog, it began to thin out.

We swatted the mist off our faces for what seemed like minutes, but then, our eyes had to adjust to the bright sun glowing above the green fields with flowers, butterflies, and pine trees.

"Santa help us, what is this place?" Patrice breathed as she bent sideways to grab a flower from the ground as the sleigh slowed down.

The layer of ice on the flower cracked and melted at Patrice's touch. "It really is frozen, flowering, and a forest! I've always believed this place was a myth!"

That was exactly how I felt when I first arrived at Candy Cane Hollow. Now, nothing could faze me. I mean, I was even engaged to Santa!

"We should pull over here," I told Nick. "The cave is high up in the mountain. But we're pretty confident Gilbert isn't in the actual cave. We should probably just get those drones running around the forest."

"You're really sure Gilbert's not in the cave?" Nick asked as he stopped the sleigh and helped Patrice and me get down.

I replied. "I'm sure; I've seen the cave – there's no way Gilbert would leave it like that. It's a huge mess!"

"Unless they tied him up," Patrice said grimly.

"I don't think they'd do that," Nick said, glancing at me knowingly. "The Yule Lads aren't violent creatures."

"Nor are they meat lovers, yet Scraper is on an all-protein diet," I pondered.

"They seem to value traditions," Nick said. "All they do is pull *harmless* pranks. And a kidnapping is harmless unless someone gets hurt, right?"

Patrice chimed in as she helped Nick prepare the drones by lining them up on the open field. "Out of all the elves, the Yule Lads seem like the most predictable bunch there are! Why do you think they steal pots and pans and not... microwaves or espresso machines? It's all about established traditions. They even live in a cave when Candy Cane Hollow has free housing projects!"

Patrice had a valid point. "I guess that's right. Although nobody could have predicted that Gilbert would be taken. They've stunned us all with this prank."

"Here," Patrice handed me and Nick controllers for the drones. Each one had a small screen attached to it. "The left joystick is used to ascend, descend, or rotate, and the right joystick is used to move the drone backward, forward, left, and right. Easy, yeah?"

"Like playing a video game," Nick said.

I knew that growing up, Nick had spent a lot of time on a sleigh riding and reindeer controlling simulation game, as every member of the Claus family had to do. No doubt flying a drone would come naturally to him. I, however, had never been much of a gamer and didn't share his confidence.

"Let's go," Patrice said, sticking her tongue out as she lifted her drone into the air with precision. I glanced at her screen and saw Patrice's camera pointed to the ground;

Patrice adjusted it, leading the drone higher and higher until it was above the tree line.

Then, Nick began controlling his drone's joysticks. "I'll go North!"

"I'll cover East and South," Patrice said, expertly controlling her drone above the towering trees, even lowering it to see through the clearings in the forest.

"I guess I'll take West," I answered. Taking responsibility for any area in the Forest made me nervous; what if I missed an area or failed to recognise a clue? I didn't want to be the reason Gilbert spent a second longer than necessary away from Claus Cottage.

To my surprise, after a few jolted attempts where my drone narrowly missed a tree and once when my finger slipped and the drone hurtled back towards the ground, I got the hang of controlling it. Just as Patrice had promised, the controls were pretty easy to work out.

The drone's mechanics whirred quietly, leaving the forest undisturbed as it flew.

I watched the screen closely, avoiding trees and leaves that could incapacitate the drone. I dipped the camera lower to look for clues – perhaps footsteps or a piece of Gilbert's clothing. But in that endless forest, it was hard to tell what could be a clue and what was simply a bright flower or a glistening piece of ice.

Although this place looked like spring, there were no birds flying above the trees or resting in branches. It was too cold. I did spot a deer and an Arctic fox, but that was about it. No signs of Gilbert yet.

The drone search continued.

At one point, my drone got caught in a tangle of branches, twigs, and leaves and couldn't be recovered.

"I'm so sorry! I'll go and fetch it," I offered. I was mortified that I had damaged something so valuable.

"We need to stay together. We can all go," Nick insisted.

Patrice shook her head and laughed. "You guys! It's just a drone. I brought plenty. Just grab another one, Holly."

"But it's... yours," I stammered.

Patrice met my gaze. "I'll happily lose a hundred drones if it means we find Gilbert."

Patrice truly was generous with her new-found wealth.

She pulled another drone out of the sleigh and rubbed my arm in encouragement.

To continue with the search, I accepted the drone and set it out on a different path. From trees with jelly beans as fruits and candy canes sprouting like flowers from the ground, I saw much that would have made me gasp with wonder on any other day.

I even stumbled upon a running river with mossy rocks of all sizes and shapes.

But no matter how many left and right turns I made with the drone, I couldn't seem to find anything related to Gilbert.

What if he wasn't here? What if we were looking at this investigation incorrectly? What if the Yule Lads weren't kidding when they said they didn't take Gilbert?

My thumbs were feeling slightly numb, so I brought the drone back to us. Plus, dusk was slowly tinting the skies with a darker shade. It was about time we headed back into town before we got lost in the freezing forest.

Nick handed hot tea from thermal flasks to Patrice and me, and I was touched by his thoughtfulness. I allowed my hand to graze his as I took my cup from him, and our eyes met. For a moment, I realised how desperate I was to marry him and call him my husband. Once we had Gilbert safely home, I was going to make wedding planning my absolute priority.

As if he could read my mind, Nick grinned at me, and the dimple in his cheek revealed itself. I felt my cheeks flush with tender love and happiness.

Then, a voice boomed from the distance and brought me back to reality. "And because I refused to sign the contract, you're opening up our forest to tourists?"

We all turned to the voice – it was Scraper with a sack of what looked like pots and pans dragging behind him in the snow. They must be the ones he stole from town! Behind him was Peeper, who gave us a small wave.

"Where's Slammer?" I asked.

Scraper shrugged as he began walking away from us, headed to the foot of the mountain. "Who knows? I'm not his owner."

"You shouldn't have left him on his own; he shouldn't be walking with a sprain."

"Then maybe you should take him in if you're so concerned. Yes, like a stray cat."

"He's not a stray cat; he's your brother."

Scraper paused from walking before turning to us slowly, still scowling. "Forgive me, doctor, but you and your family don't seem like the kind of people who care about who and what we are. Remember? You've turned us Yule Lads into domesticated cavemen!"

Patrice hid behind my leg, intimidated by Scraper's strong looks and sharp words.

As Scraper and Peeper continued walking, Nick shouted behind them. "Just tell us where Gilbert is, and we'll leave!"

This time, Scraper didn't stop walking; he just continued heading to the mountain.

Now, I had to worry about Slammer, too. If he tried to

walk all this way to the forest, he'd definitely hurt his ankle more.

Nick couldn't bear to just watch Scraper and Peeper leave, so he handed me his controller. "I'll talk some sense into him—"

Before Nick could even take a step to follow Scraper, his phone rang. And so, he pulled his phone out of his pocket, showing me the caller ID.

It was Mrs Claus.

For some reason, I found myself holding my breath.

"Hello, Mum? Everything all right?" Nick answered the phone.

I watched him listen to Mrs Claus – his expression changed from concern to fear. His back heaved as he took a deep breath that unsettled me.

As he put down his phone, Nick avoided my gaze. His dimple was long gone. "Mum wants us back home."

"Did something happen?" My voice almost got caught in my mouth.

Nick's expression warned me that I was not going to like the news; I wished I could read his mind to brace myself for his words.

"They've found something in Gilbert's room."

# 12

The sleigh ride back to Claus Cottage was blurry in my head, but I probably had inhaled so much cold air that my mind was making no sense.

I'd like to think that good news awaited us at home, but I could tell from Nick's tensed jaws as he gritted his teeth that something was wrong.

Nick and I were silent after dropping Patrice at the High Street and promising to give her an update about Gilbert as soon as we could. We could only nod and give weak waves to passers-by, who greeted us with hearty rounds of wishing us a Merry Christmas.

Despite all the Christmas lights twinkling and dancing, the stars glowing overhead, the Christmas songs playing in every house and establishment, and even the smell of food wafting in the air, I didn't feel merry at all.

The night sky only indicated how we had burned through the day without finding Gilbert. Our efforts were futile. And now we were coming home to what I knew was bad news.

When we got to Claus Cottage, Nick and I hurried back inside, bracing ourselves for the worst.

I had locked out the voices in my head whispering worst-case scenarios – I wasn't ready for any of them, so I didn't want to hear them.

Before opening the front door, Nick took my hand.

I didn't even think I needed to be comforted until his warm hand wrapped over mine. I was glad he was here with me for whatever we were about to discover.

Nick opened the door, and we finally stepped in. While I expected the living room floor to have split open, revealing the earth's core or some other tragedy, the room was empty. The earth's crust hadn't penetrated the wooden floors.

"Holly!" August's head popped out from the kitchen hallway, rocking little Jeb in her arms. "Over here."

Nick and I headed that way without pause or delay, although I really wanted to stop so I could just get my breathing to return to normal. But it helped that Nick was going through the same thing as me.

We dashed down the hallway before finally arriving at the kitchen.

Right there and then, I hated myself for thinking I would find Gilbert... lifeless. So, it was still a relief to find only a piece of paper in Mrs Claus' left hand. In her right hand was a handkerchief she was using to wipe her cheeks. She had been crying.

Father Christmas stood behind Mrs Claus, Tom leaned by the sink, and Gwen was hugging her knees in the corner of the room. It was a depressing scene.

Nick rushed to his mother's side while I found myself unable to take another step without his hands on mine.

Standing next to August, I whispered. "What's happening?"

I could tell from the lines on August's forehead that she didn't want to say anything to me. So, I watched Nick mumble something to Mrs Claus.

Mrs Claus handed Nick the paper; I watched his eyes move as he read through the lines. Then, he let out a shaky breath... like someone had knocked the air out of his lungs.

"What is it?" I asked. My voice was a little too loud in the cottage's silence and I cringed at the sound of it.

"You should look at this, Holly," Nick walked back to me, the paper between us.

I reached for the flimsy and grainy page with a shaking hand, immediately recognising Gilbert's handwriting.

I would know because his letter A's looked like half-eaten pretzels, and his letter O's had a curved line in the middle.

It read:


*I don't know how to say this in person, so I'm leaving a note instead.*
*For an elf, I have outgrown this place.*
*I no longer fit in here, so I'm off to somewhere better.*
*Love, Gilbert*


I read the six lines two or three times as if I had forgotten how to read. But even if I read it three dozen times, it still didn't make sense to me.

"Gilbert couldn't have written this," was the first thing I said after the shock wore off. "It's impossible! He loved this place. He loved serving all of us. He loved serving you, Mrs Claus."

Waving the paper in the air like it couldn't be Gilbert's

final note, I continued. "Gilbert would never write something like this. How did you even find this all of a sudden?"

"It was me," Gwen squeaked, raising her hand. "Call it nosy, but I really wanted to help after you all nursed me back to health. I also wanted to look for Gilbert. I thought I might find a clue in his bedroom, but instead, I found that on his study table."

My hand gripped a bit too tightly on the sheet of paper.

Of course, we couldn't have seen it. We hadn't even looked in his room in the first place. Because we knew how much Gilbert valued his privacy, and there was just no way he'd leave a note like this.

Sensing my frustration, Nick gently grabbed my hand with the paper. "Holly, we know what you feel. This isn't like him at all. But that handwriting..."

"It's his," Mrs Claus confirmed. "In the last hour, I have been fooling myself into thinking that it wasn't Gilbert's handwriting – that it looked a little bit off, but maybe there's a reason why we can't find him."

*Because he doesn't want to be found?* I couldn't bring myself to say that out loud. Instead, I shook my head. "Don't say that, Mrs Claus. This doesn't make sense!"

"No?" Mrs Claus' voice sounded like she wanted me to change her mind.

And I happily would.

I wasn't going to let her give up on Gilbert.

"Because no one just changes their minds or their feelings overnight," I explained, trying not to make this make sense. "Gilbert went out to grab groceries to make burgers for Angel Albright, his idol! No one would get groceries before disappearing."

"Maybe he wanted to make it look like he was kidnapped?" Tom replied, trying to be rational about it.

Easy for him; he barely knew Gilbert. He couldn't possibly be emotional about it. I immediately felt ashamed of my harshness towards my brother-in-law. Of course he was emotional. He was a good man.

"But why leave a note?" I responded, making what I felt was a good point. "Look, Gilbert wouldn't even leave the house without his measuring cups, let alone his cookware! Like that one, what is it, he had been gazing at it in the catalogue for months..."

"Oh, yes. His enamel cast iron cookware," Mrs Claus elaborated with a smile.

"Yes! That one!" I called, remembering Gilbert telling me about its durability, non-toxicity, and double use for stovetop and oven cooking. He even had its handles personalised with the first letter of his name.

Just then, I also remembered one thing he said. "I can prove he didn't write this. Since he loved that new cookware so much, I'm sure he wouldn't have left it behind if he had really left voluntarily! Gilbert told me he left it under his bed, so it was close to him for cuddling!"

I probably sounded frantic at that moment, like a mad woman preaching that Santa Claus and the Bogeyman were the same people in different suits, but I didn't care.

I even felt encouraged by seeing Mrs Claus rise from her chair. So, I took the lead and walked down the hall, just across the kitchen. There was the small, nondescript door that housed Gilbert's quarters.

I raced towards it, hearing my heart beat in my eardrums as I closed in on it.

Behind me were footsteps from the rest of the group, all waiting for me to prove myself right. Or wrong.

Once I found that cookware, they'd know I was right.

Facing Gilbert's door, for a split second I heard a voice of doubt inside me. Perhaps I was wrong. Gilbert had threatened to hang up his apron and leave us many times, maybe he had finally decided to actually do it. But, I refused to waver. So, I ignored the fear on my shoulder and opened the bedroom door.

It was a space I had never been in before. Gilbert was incredibly private about his personal space, and kept his bedroom door locked. While he would have never outwardly said that his room was out of bounds, it was understood by everyone at Claus Cottage that that was the case.

Entering his room without his knowledge felt like a betrayal, but I reminded myself that I was only doing it to try and help him.

I bent down a little to squeeze myself into the cramped room, then knelt down on the floor to check under Gilbert's bed.

I was sure it'd be right there, waiting for Gilbert to use it again. Or even hug it again during one of his frequent kitchen-related nightmares. But as I peered through the space between the bed and the floor, I was surprised to find it empty. Not even a single speck of dust lay there.

"It might be more easy if I looked, Holly," Gwen spoke behind me.

Although I didn't see anything under the bed, I backed away and returned to the hall, watching Gwen search under the bed for the cookware Gilbert loved so dearly.

With her smaller frame, Gwen managed to slip half of her body under the bed with ease.

Finally, Gwen slid out from under the furniture.

With not so much as a cobweb stuck to her hair, she shook her head. "I didn't find anything. This cookware that you're talking about, it's not here."

My heart plummeted to my stomach.

How could that be?

Why would that be?

I felt a hand rub my back, and it was Mrs Claus. Still with tears in her eyes, she said. "We better prepare some dinner, dear. It's Jeb's first Christmas here in Candy Cane Hollow, and you don't want to send Nick on his traditional sleigh ride on an empty stomach, do you?"

It all felt surreal.

Even as I nodded to Mrs Claus and the group dispersed from the hallway, I found myself staring back at Gilbert's tidy room, still hoping he'd pop his head behind the door and give me an earful for peeking without his permission.

As the group disappeared into the kitchen, Nick stayed with me.

Touching my shoulder, Nick slowly moved my body so we'd be facing each other. He looked at me with heavy eyes as he said. "It's going to be alright, Holly."

I closed my eyes and let myself believe Nick – believe Santa. Maybe he had some Christmas magic up in his sleeve.

Then, Nick pulled me into a comforting embrace.

## 13

A part from the sound of kitchenware and utensils clanging into each other here and there, Claus Cottage was quiet. The house was enveloped by a devastating kind of silence that only Gilbert's absence could create.

Since our Christmas dinner was a few hours later than usual, each one of us was tasked with making our own dish – like a potluck – out of one of Mrs Claus' cookbooks.

I thought Mrs Claus had opted to do that so we could all be distracted from the shocking and devastating news. If so, she was right; I needed to keep busy with something else, or I might just break down.

Gilbert was a great friend to me.

Seeing Mrs Claus cook her Beef Wellington beside Father Christmas, who was tasked with putting together the winter salad, I felt ashamed that I couldn't pull myself together as well as Mrs Claus did.

She must have been more heartbroken than I was, yet she was working on tonight's main course effortlessly.

As for me, I was making apple crisps for dessert with a

rather straightforward recipe. I guessed that was why this was given to me; it would be hard to mess up putting together sliced apples, sugar, flour, cinnamon, and oats.

I'd probably still mess it up, given how distracted I was, so I was putting in extra effort to line up the unevenly sliced apples in the baking dish.

August, a more seasoned cook than I was, was working on the green bean casserole. Tom and Jeb were upstairs for a nappy change followed by a nap. Nick was exempted from cooking because he had to be in his best shape for the night's sleigh ride.

Finally, Gwen worked on what she claimed was her signature dish of mini mushroom and goat cheese tarts, plus an easy-made cranberry brie bite for appetisers.

Unlike all of us, Gwen barely felt Gilbert's absence – how could she? She hadn't been here before. In fact, she was the only one who was humming among the group. Perhaps it was her innate love for Christmas as an elf. Or her love of providing domestic help, which was innate in every house elf.

Hearing Gwen hum off-tune made me miss Gilbert's sassy and uptight self even more. Sure, Gwen seemed eager to help and positively cheery, but Gilbert's attitude whenever he worked in the kitchen was loved by all of us.

It wasn't the same without him.

But what if it wasn't going to be the same anymore?

*Snap out of it, Holly.* I scolded myself, turning my attention to the apples again.

"You okay there?" August must have noticed my frustration as she slid towards me.

"I'm just making sure this dessert will be perfect." I lied. Honestly, I didn't care about the meal at all.

"It doesn't have to be," August smiled at me. "I think the

essence of Christmas is this – all of us cooking together. It's nice, don't you think?"

I looked around the room once more.

If I didn't focus on Gilbert being nowhere in sight, it really was a heartwarming scene. Mrs Claus and Father Christmas were working shoulder to shoulder, my sister was by my side, and even Gwen added a touch of cheer since her Christmas spirit hadn't wavered like the rest of ours had.

Perhaps I could pretend this was still a good Christmas night.

I could try.

So, I tried.

Within two hours, we had set up the dinner table with a full four-course meal.

"You all made this?" Nick walked towards the dining room with a new, cleaner Santa suit – the one he'd be wearing for tonight's sleigh ride. And he looked good in it, too.

His dimple showed as he smiled at the table filled with food we had prepared.

I found myself gravitating to his side. "I made those apple crisps."

Nick's eyes shifted towards the well-baked apple crisps. Ultimately, I didn't end up burning the whole cottage down with my cooking skills. Perhaps I should start learning how to cook under Mrs Claus' direction.

But wouldn't that mean I was no longer expecting Gilbert to come home and do the cooking?

I didn't want to know the answer to that.

Nick pulled me closer to him with a proud smile. "It looks delicious, Holly."

I blushed, still as enamoured with Nick as the first day we had met here at Claus Cottage, and I was just a certain 'waif and stray' that Mrs Claus took in after I had hit my car in a snowbank in London.

"Gather around, everyone!" Father Christmas' voice boomed out as he extended his arms over the meal we had before us. "We better dig in while everything's fresh and hot."

Everyone took their seats dutifully, a mixture of exhaustion and slight hunger etched on our faces.

I sat between Nick and August. Father Christmas was at the head of the table; to his right was Mrs Claus, and Nick was to his left. Beside Gwen was Jeb in a high chair with a silicon plate of spinach mashed potato, then Tom.

And right at the other end of the table was an empty seat.

An empty seat with a clean plate and utensils lined up neatly as if someone would occupy it.

It was apparent we hoped Gilbert would join us.

I wasn't the only one seeing the glaring space on the table, but all of us ignored it. It was probably better off that way, at least for now.

I swore that I would return to looking for Gilbert in the morning. But for now, I passed on the dishes to the rest of the group while we ate in silence.

"So, the traditional sleigh ride," August slightly adjusted herself forward to address Nick. "How does that go? I was thinking of letting Jeb witness it first-hand, you know? After all, it's his first Christmas here."

When it came to Jeb, August had always been a wonder woman of a mother, but she had been more at ease with parenting since she got here. Maybe it was because her husband had an understanding boss who refused to make him work overtime and who wasn't strict about attendance as long as Tom got the job done.

August now had her husband helping her with Jeb for more hours compared to when they were in London.

I wasn't surprised that even with Gilbert missing, August's focus was on giving Jeb an incredible experience.

It was every child's dream, surely.

Frankly, who was the better person to ask about it than Santa himself?

Nick swallowed his food first before answering. "Well, at midnight, I ride my sleigh with the reindeer, including the infamous Rudolph of course, and we set off to the sky, ride around for hours through city skies."

"Fast as lightning, no one could really witness it," Father Christmas added. "At least for those outside of Candy Cane Hollow."

"You could see the sleigh taking off from the balcony," I suggested, thinking it was the only way to do it. It wasn't like there was a private viewing room to watch Santa's sleigh take off...right?

"It's been a long, harrowing day, and I don't mind taking that little one to the Santa HQ's helipad." Mrs Claus wiggled her point finger to Jeb, who laughed soundlessly.

I turned to Nick. "The sleigh takes off from a helipad?"

This was the first time I had heard that.

Nick shrugged his shoulders shyly. "Well, a small airstrip would've cost us more for a sleigh, so we stuck to the helipad."

"You *considered* building a small airstrip?"

"Well, we had to consider everything..."

"So, can we all go to Santa HQ and watch the sleigh take off?" August asked excitedly. "Jeb would be delighted!"

I was sure it wasn't just Jeb who would be delighted; it was also August herself, who had been a full-on Christmas fanatic since birth. I could still remember her leaving out

milk and cookies for Santa Claus every Christmas Eve when
we were growing up.

Looking at August's cheery expression, only a heartless
person could say no to that. And as expected, Father
Christmas laughed. "It's been a while since we brought
guests to the traditional sleigh ride. Let's do it."

THE SANTA HQ vibrated with life in a symphony of chaos –
elves scurried on the production floor as they made final
checks on all the gifts for all the kids on the nice list.

Machines whirred endlessly, printing the last few
receipts with delivery details before the sleigh took off.

The traditional sleigh ride was the highlight of a year's
incredibly hard work, and there was an even higher buzz of
anticipation among everyone at Santa HQ.

As we walked through the building, August bounced on
the balls of her feet. She was practically floating, she was so
excited.

August cooed and explained to Jeb what they were looking
at, although Jeb probably only liked the colours and the lights.

All the elves might be busy, but they still grinned and
greeted us as we passed them by.

Nick didn't fail to tell them they were doing well and
thank them for their hard work.

Soon, we rode the lift towards the top floor, leaving only
one flight of stairs leading up to the rooftop.

As we got there, more elves awaited Nick.

I could see their surprise as Father Christmas and more
unexpected guests walked behind Nick, but they kept their
composure.

The elves formed two lines, making an aisle that led to the sleigh.

August gasped when she set her eyes on Rudolph, who was at the head of the group of reindeer. He was an elegant, regal looking creature, taller than the other reindeer by about a foot. If it was possible for a reindeer to have confidence, Rudolph had plenty of it.

"We sing about him, remember?" August asked Jeb while pointing at Rudolph with his distinctive red nose.

"Wow..." Gwen slurred as she looked around the impressive sight.

Every elf stood still in line like soldiers at Buckingham Palace; in their hands was a gold stick with red and green ribbons swirling around the handle. At the end of the stick, at least twenty bells were waiting to be rung.

*Those must be the Christmas bells I heard from the balcony to signal Santa's take-off!*

It was incredibly exciting to see everything unfold.

"This is where the magic happens," Nick turned around to tell us.

I grinned at him, sensing he was nervous. He probably hadn't had guests watch him do this before.

Nick glanced at his wristwatch, and I peered over his shoulder, which was just a few seconds before midnight.

*Tick, tock, tick, tock.*

*Tick...*the clock hand struck midnight.

That was when the door behind us opened, and Mitzy, in a fancier uniform than normal, appeared. She carried a velvet box in her tiny hands.

We split into two groups to let her pass.

Mitzy carried the box towards Nick elegantly, then finally opened it and presented his Santa hat.

"May your Christmas be merry and your ride be safe," Mitzy said with a bow as she offered the open velvet box.

Nick carefully took the exquisite-looking Santa hat, which was made of materials unlike those from any store I had ever been in, and put it over his head like a crown. He replied. "May our ride be safe."

With that, the elves in line all rang their bells at the same time, sending a sweet Christmas tune to our ears. The bells' music travelled to the reindeers' ears; they perked and whinnied in attention as Nick ceremoniously walked the aisle toward his sleigh.

Before climbing aboard, however, Nick walked to Rudolph.

With a touch of his finger to the reindeer's nose, it glowed bright red like there was a switch.

Everyone held their breaths as the bells continued ringing and as Nick climbed the sleigh.

As he settled in, it was like the sleigh came alive. Runes that I didn't notice earlier nor could decipher glowed gold on the polished redwood. It rumbled for a moment, then slowly, the runners lifted from the rooftop.

There was no strong wind like a chopper normally would have; instead, there was snow – like a snow machine running underneath the sleigh.

For a second or two, the sleigh hung suspended in the air. Then, it slowly ascended into the sky with Nick laughing, 'Ho, ho, ho!' and wishing everyone a Merry Christmas.

As the sleigh climbed higher into the thick clouds, a burst of white light shot it forward; it wasn't a strong launch but rather a ripple to the fabric of reality itself. Perhaps.

The ripple left a white glow in the clouds, followed by snow swirling down beautifully to Candy Cane Hollow.

It was a sight unlike any other.

It brought tears to my eyes – and to August's.

I embraced her sideways, realising the power of this moment for her.

In those precious moments, I almost fooled myself into thinking that nothing was wrong. But it was just a fleeting moment.

I still had to find Gilbert.

## 14

Despite the bone-aching tiredness I felt across my whole body, I jolted awake sometime before sunrise.

It was like my whole body was repulsed by the thought of oversleeping when Gilbert was still missing.

After last night's unexpected visit to Santa HQ to watch the sleigh ride, the weight of the world on my shoulders was eased by all the magic I witnessed. I was already asleep before I could even toss and turn on my bed.

Knowing I had a mission, I groggily tried to move out of bed but was stopped by a weight around my hips.

Adjusting to my side, I realised it was Nick, snuggled in bed with me, seemingly in a deep sleep brought about by an outer-body kind of exhaustion that knocked him out on my bed.

I was guessing he snuck into my bedroom when he came home and didn't intend to sleep next to me, but he probably fell asleep in an instant after his long night of hard work.

Mrs Claus would tease us all day if she found out... or at least she would if this was any ordinary day.

I took the chance to gaze at Nick's soft features for a moment. Who knew that the next generation Santa would be a hunk?

Running a finger on the side of his face, I realised I could get used to waking up with him every morning just like this once we were married.

As if Nick could hear my thoughts, he suddenly mumbled sleepily. "We should pick a wedding date soon."

Was he dreaming about me and our wedding? Was he trying to converse with me while he was half-asleep?

Either way, I answered him with a whisper. "We'll do that after we find Gilbert, okay?"

"Hmm..." Nick answered with his eyes heavy and shut.

I watched his chest rise and fall as he fell back into sleep.

Being Santa was a full-time job, and he worked all year round because a year's worth of wishes worldwide couldn't possibly be accomplished in one night. While last night was the busiest night of the year, Nick's mind would already be looking ahead to the next Christmas when he woke.

After a while, I carefully slid out of Nick's arms, feeling sorry I couldn't stay in bed with him longer. But my guilt outweighed that feeling – I had to know that Gilbert was safe.

If he really had chosen to leave, I had to know he did it with the best intentions. Although he'd be getting an earful from me if he really did leave without talking to his employer. And his friends, like me and August.

I wasn't proud to admit it, but I would take his sudden departure without notice personally. Yes, I would be saddened *and* offended.

I put on warmer, more comfortable clothes before leaving my bedroom, leaving Nick peacefully asleep and undisturbed.

I had no idea where to start after being stumped by the note Gwen found in Gilbert's bedroom. Should I call Wiggles and Cornelius? Tell them to stop the search? Should I ask them to raise the alarms because we were potentially dealing with a meticulous kidnapper who might've been inside Claus Cottage?

Still, it was Christmas morning, and I refused to ring either Wiggles or Cornelius so early in the morning.

They had already spent Christmas Eve searching for Gilbert; they deserved to sleep in and wake up to the scent of cinnamon and pine. Hot chocolate, too.

Speaking of hot chocolate, I should make one for myself since I was the only person awake in the house.

I descended the stairs leading to the common room to make my way straight to the kitchen. But as I walked past the windows, I noticed a figure sitting on the cottage's doorstep.

I rubbed my eyes to ensure I wasn't dreaming... but a Yule Lad was sitting out there!

Hurriedly, I unlocked the front door and opened it; the cold wind immediately hit my skin like it would freeze and crack within seconds.

I was right! A Yule Lad was sitting up front, now looking up at me. "Doctor..."

It was Slammer – the Yule Lad who I had treated for a sprain.

"Slammer, what are you doing here?" I asked him, worried as I looked at his bandaged ankle and the crutch lying on his side.

Slammer stood up with the help of his crutch. "I was hoping I could speak to someone from this household. Ideally you, if you don't mind."

Although I doubted Slammer was cold since he had

such thick skin and years of living in the Frozen Flowering Forest with nothing but a bonfire to keep him warm in the cave, I still escorted him inside as quickly as I could.

"Come on in," I said.

"Thank you," Slammer replied politely.

I closed the door behind us and led him to the kitchen, where I immediately boiled some water. "I'll make us some hot chocolates."

"With peppermint, please, if you don't mind," Slammer added.

"I'm sure we have peppermint candy canes in one of these cupboards. Would that work?"

"Even better than those organic leaves!"

"Alright," I began searching in the candy cupboard. "So, why did you come all the way here, Slammer?"

"Erm..." Slammer wiggled in his seat uncomfortably. "I don't know if I should tell you this, but I've been thinking about your missing elf, Gilly."

"Close, but it's Gilbert," I informed him.

"Right, Gilbert." Slammer paused. "You see, while we're known liars, you have to believe me when I tell you that we don't have your missing elf."

Something about the way Slammer said it made me actually believe him. Or was I a fool to believe a Yule Lad?

Yet, why would a Yule Lad who could hardly walk come all the way here just to lie? That made less sense than believing a Yule Lad was being honest for once.

I ought to give Slammer the benefit of the doubt. "Okay, I'll believe you. But I bet you didn't come all this way to just say that, right?"

"Of course," Slammer slurred, hesitating. He even looked around the room and scanned the surrounding windows as if he was worried about something.

"What is it, Slammer?" I said with a calm tone. "If you're in trouble, you can tell me. This is one of the safest places in Candy Cane Hollow."

"I guess you're right. But I can't help but feel nervous, especially since I've never done this before."

"Done what before?"

Just as Slammer was about to open his mouth in response, the kettle hissed as it boiled.

I swiftly turned off the stovetop and carefully poured the hot water into mugs – which Gilbert would scold me for. He would've been furious if he saw me make hot chocolate with water... again.

Still, I kept sloppily mixing water with chocolate and added a peppermint candy cane to Slammer's mug.

I slid the steaming mug of the hot chocolate to Slammer, getting right back to the conversation. "You were saying?"

Slammer wrapped his hands in the hot porcelain. "It's Scraper. Since yesterday, he has been holed up in his private hut down at the Rink River past No Carols Cave."

I listened to him thoughtfully. "And why is that concerning?"

Slammer took a sip of his hot chocolate. "It's not odd that Scraper disappears into his hut occasionally, but he always comes home. Last night, he spent the night there, and all of us Yule Lads are worried that he's done something terrible and is in hiding."

I felt my breath hitch. "Do you have any idea what he might've done?"

Slammer averted his gaze from me ruefully. "I think it has something to do with your missing elf."

## 15

The sun cast a golden light onto the hallways as I raced to my bedroom to grab a coat and a scarf for my early morning adventure with Slammer.

But, of course, nothing was adventurous about facing the most menacing Yule Lad in all of Candy Cane Hollow. The thought made me queasy. To make matters worse, he might even be the kidnapper we had been looking for.

As quietly as I could, I entered my bedroom and tiptoed to my closet.

I didn't want to wake Nick – nor anybody else in this house.

I figured yesterday's events had been too emotional for all of us, and they all deserved a break from worrying too much. I was sure they could use a slow Christmas morning, as Christmas mornings were supposed to be.

Before I alarmed anyone else with this 'tip' against Scraper from a fellow Yule Lad, I had to ensure it would lead us somewhere. Blindly searching for Gilbert had been an emotional rollercoaster already.

Breaking such alarming news before 7AM felt too cruel, especially if it turned out to be another dead end.

Quietly, I grabbed the first coat and scarf I could reach from my cabinet, then snuck out of the room again.

Nick was too tired to notice as I came and went. *Phew.*

As I raced down the stairs, I realised I had grabbed a yellow coat and pink scarf – two colours I couldn't possibly pull off together. Still, I wore them, more concerned about discovering what Scraper had really been up to than worrying about my outfit.

Slammer patiently waited for me at the bottom of the stairs.

In a semi-whisper, I asked him. "You can lead me to Frozen Flowering Forest, right? Because I heard only the Clauses can pierce through the magical mist hiding that forest in plain sight."

"Clauses *and* the Yule Lads," Slammer informed me. "As long as you're accompanied by one of those two, the mist will appear to you as an entrance. If not, it's nothing but a thick fog."

I still didn't understand how that worked, but this wasn't the time for that. I told Slammer. "You and I can head to the Rink River, then. Come on. I'll go get a sleigh ready –"

"Ready for what?" A pointed voice echoed behind me, making the hair on the back of my neck stand up.

I immediately recognised that voice – Mrs Claus.

Slowly, I turned around, thinking about an excuse for why I was heading out with a Yule Lad. I could say I was trying to destress by giving stomping on people's roofs a try? But I had always been a bad liar. So, I said. "It's nothing to worry about; Slammer and I were just, um..."

"Headed to the Rink River to find Scraper because we

think he kidnapped Gilly," Slammer answered quickly and breathlessly.

As I turned to him with horror, Slammer's hands flew over his mouth.

"You mean Gilbert?" Mrs Claus replied; her voice might have sounded calm, but her expression was grim. Maybe even disappointed, as she told me. "I hope you weren't trying to withhold this information from me, Holly."

"I... I wasn't!" I stammered, then confessed. "I was going to tell you after I confirmed Slammer's speculations."

"That sounds sensible," Mrs Claus nodded with her eyes closed, immediately relieving me. She added. "Let me go grab my coat. I'm coming with you. And you're right; we shouldn't tell anyone else."

I couldn't argue with Mrs Claus, and I didn't want to. Some friendly company would be nice, I had to admit.

I smiled at Slammer sheepishly. "Looks like Mrs Claus is coming with us."

"JUST STRAIGHT AHEAD," Slammer pointed as we passed by the foot of the mountain that would lead us to No Carols Cave. But this time, we were sleighing right past it.

As I looked at the jagged rocks with all the cracks and crevices that could house who knows what – I shuddered a little at how unsettling the mountain actually was.

It was tall and full of mysteries, filled with lichen and ice on most surfaces.

You could hardly see the opening of No Carols Cave from the bottom.

The entire place was, as always, cold and peaceful. By peaceful, I meant *eerily* quiet. You shouldn't be fooled by the spring-like façade of it all – there were no birds singing and only frozen insects.

It was an uninhabitable place. Unwelcoming and unkind.

This was a place Gilbert wouldn't survive a day in. And perhaps that was what made the entire thing so scary.

Slammer led us in a straight line for a few miles. Soon, we headed inside the stomach of a forest with only white pine trees with white-coloured tree trunks and branches.

The very definition of a white Christmas, except it looked colourless and bland.

The Frozen Flowering Forest was slowly losing its appeal to me.

"We should probably leave the sleigh around here and go on foot," Slammer suggested.

"But your foot..." the doctor in me quickly intervened. "You should take it easy on your sprained ankle."

"It's alright," Slammer assured me. "It'd be better if we attract less attention... and if Scraper didn't know I led you to his private hut."

I glanced at Mrs Claus, who was focused on finding a spot to park the sleigh. "He'd think you betrayed him, huh?"

"And all hell would break loose," Slammer spoke grimly.

Mrs Claus slowly stopped in a small clearing, where we could hear the river running. She turned around to scold Slammer. "Don't say that, dear. I'm sure Scraper would understand why you did it."

Slammer shivered in fear. "I think I'd prefer if he didn't know at all. I wouldn't want to mess up the universe's balance by breaking up the Yule Lads."

"Mess up the universe's balance?" I parroted. "That seems... a bit overdramatic, don't you think?"

"No, no. It's true," Mrs Claus answered with a blank

expression. "It hasn't happened in a century, but rumour has it that if the thirteen Yule Lads ever break up, Candy Cane Hollow would suffer the same fate as the Frozen Flowering Forest. No Christmas lights would twinkle, no carols would be heard, and no joyous Christmas spirit would ever break the curse until all thirteen of them, or at least their predecessors, would reconcile."

It was my turn to shiver. I replied. "Well, if you put it that way, it seems smarter if Scraper doesn't see us until we have a plan that won't incriminate the Yule Lads."

"That's right," Mrs Claus gracefully hopped out of the sleigh. "Now, we should see that up-to-no-good Scraper for ourselves."

"Okay..." I nodded, helping Slammer off the sleigh.

This time, Mrs Claus led the way by simply following the sound of running water, the steady thrum of the rapids, and the gurgling hum of pebbles tossing at the current under the riverbed.

After a short walk, we finally found the river. But for some reason, it wasn't running at all. The surface was solidly frozen, which would explain why it was called the Rink River – the surface might as well be a skating rink judging by the thickened ice above.

But under the crystallised surface, water did run just as any river did.

Unexplainable. Impressive.

Beyond the river was another snowy hill with frozen green trees; even the wind couldn't shake them.

"It's over there," Slammer pointed to a group of rocks and boulders of all shapes and sizes covered with more lichen sitting near the riverbank. "It's a stone hut. If you head straight that way, you'll find Scraper's hut perched on top of some other boulders. But it blends in well, so keep your eyes peeled."

Mrs Claus began walking that way, but I paused to look at Slammer. "How about you?"

"It'd be best if I stay here; if Scraper is there, I could hide."

"Right, well make sure you hide well," I said mostly to myself.

I began following Mrs Claus towards the rocks, her eyes searching for a hut-looking rock among other semi-identical rocks.

It didn't take long for her sharp eyes to find Scraper's hut.

"There," Mrs Claus pointed to her right. A moss-covered stone hut with jagged stones for walls, a tiny chimney peeking at the back, and a whimsical topiary tree atop its roof greeted us.

It looked like a figurine I could buy from a fairy shop. It even had lamps hanging by the door filled with fireflies rather than fire.

Despite its smaller structure, it could definitely fit one of us. So, I volunteered. "I'll go check inside, Mrs Claus."

Mrs Claus didn't argue. "Be careful, dear. You should probably try knocking first; maybe Scraper will be in a better mood now and want to talk."

I nodded.

I walked closer to the stone hut, climbing the rocks a little to get closer to the door. Upon getting there, I gently knocked on the door. "Hello? Anyone home?"

I waited for a few seconds, but no one came to the door, so I tried the door handle. Without much effort, the door opened with a click.

I glanced at Mrs Claus, who gestured at me to go in, and I did.

Bending my head a little, I stepped into the cosy abode.

Still with jagged rocks for walls, the room was spacious; there were no other bedrooms or doors. It had a table and chairs, even a coffee table and a bookshelf, all seemingly handmade.

What caught my eye the most were all the pots and pans hanging on the ceiling and on one side of the wall. They also covered almost any other surface in the room apart from the floor. Presumably, I was looking at all of the pots and pans that Scraper had stolen.

The soft glow came from more fireflies kept in glass jars hung around the room.

At first glance, nothing seemed out of the ordinary. I continued looking around, risking a pinched nerve in my neck as I hunched over the room.

There were no hidden doors on the walls or hidden compartments on the floor. Basically, there was nowhere to hide Gilbert.

There was no sign of Gilbert whatsoever.

Relief and dismay brewed in my chest. At this point, any sign of Gilbert would be nice.

Not knowing where he was and if he was okay was a much scarier thing to deal with.

I still wasn't convinced he had left on his own volition.

Just as I turned to leave, I caught a glimpse of fabric from my periphery. Turning to look at it, I realised it was a navy blue carry-on bag, much like the one Gilbert kept under his bed.

I missed Gilbert.

*Wait...*my brain suddenly went into overload. Was I looking at Gilbert's bag?

My heart began pounding before I even got the chance to inspect the familiar bag closer. My hands shook as I crouched down and reached for it, sliding the heavy bag closer to me.

Could this really be Gilbert's bag?

There was only one way to find out.

My fingers closed on the zipper, and I began zipping the bag open; a part of me hoped it was Gilbert's, but a part of me also hoped it wasn't. It was a confusing feeling – wanting to know where Gilbert was and not wanting to know at all in case he was in distress, and I couldn't bear it.

Soon, the bag was fully open. And there inside was a beautiful set of enamel cast iron cookware.

It could've been a coincidence that Scraper, known for his innate attraction to pots and pans, had the same cookware. But as I pulled out a pan, I saw the letter G engraved on the handle.

It was Gilbert's.

## 16

Mrs Claus stared at the open bag with Gilbert's most treasured cookware inside. I could tell by her dilating pupils that she knew it belonged to Gilbert without a doubt.

I had taken the bag to where we parked the sleigh so we'd be away from Scraper in case he returned to his hut.

"What should we do?" I asked Mrs Claus.

Mrs Claus continued ogling the bag, her mind running on its full rotors. I could almost hear the mechanical whir.

On the other side of the sleigh, Slammer bit at his nails nervously. "Were we right? Did Scraper really kidnap that poor elf?"

I sighed. "I don't know, but this bag belonged to Gilbert."

"First..." Mrs Claus suddenly spoke. "Let's return this bag to the hut; we don't want to alert Scraper that we're on his tail while we figure out what to do next."

I bent down to close the bag and carried it over my shoulder. "I'll return it. I'll be back in a jiffy."

Since we were conveniently parked near the river, it was

easy to navigate the same path we took leading to the stone hut.

I made sure to look around before sneaking inside Scraper's hut again. Then, I returned the bag right where I found it, hesitating for a second. This was a special piece of cookware to Gilbert. It seemed wrong to leave it in the hut. It felt almost like a betrayal.

Immediately snapping out of it, I left the hut and ran back to the woods where Mrs Claus was in deep thought.

"I think Scraper is too unpredictable at the moment. Maybe even a little angry. It might be dangerous for us to confront him on our own, Holly."

Considering that Scraper might be a kidnapper, dangerous wasn't a farfetched word to describe him with. "I agree, Mrs Claus. Should we call Wiggles and Cornelius?"

"Wiggles and Cornelis?" Slammer said with a hiccup. "Aren't they... police officers? Are you turning over Scraper to the police? That would mess up the universe's balance!"

"I don't think it will, dear," Mrs Claus replied with a motherly tone. "As long as Scraper doesn't find out you're working with us, he couldn't possibly hate you or the Yule Lads! The only balance he's messing with is the scales of Lady Justice."

"I'm not working with you!" Slammer huffed. "I'm just... entertaining you as the forest's guests!"

"Of course," I winked at Slammer, understanding his cue. "You're just being hospitable."

"It'd be best if Slammer returns to No Carols Cave before Wiggles and Cornelius get here. I'm sure they won't ask too many questions about how we found the hut."

"We could say we stumbled upon it by chance while searching the forest. After all, Nick, Patrice, and I were here yesterday. It wouldn't be suspicious that we're here now."

"Alright, we could stick to that story." Mrs Claus turned to Slammer. "As for you, young elf, you should hurry back to your cave. Don't tell anyone you entertained us like the courteous elf that you are."

Slammer blushed a little at Mrs Claus' kind remark. "I'll see you around, Mrs Claus. And you, Doc."

As Slammer began walking with his crutch, I shouted behind him. "Should we give you a ride?"

"I'll be fine!" He shouted back. "This is a mystical forest; the wind will take me home!"

Clearly, I had little understanding of how this forest worked. Mrs Claus and I watched Slammer trudge carefully across the snow until, sure enough, his walking increased in pace until it almost looked as if he was being carried by the wind.

"I'll ring Wiggles now," Mrs Claus said.

I couldn't imagine her being about to get a phone signal. As if sensing my doubt, she gave me a reassuring smile. "Wiggles' phone is ringing."

I simply nodded, waiting for Mrs Claus to do the talking.

After a few seconds, she pulled the phone away. "Let me try Cornelius' number..."

We both waited in anticipation as Cornelius' line rang.

I knew it was barely eight on Christmas morning, but wouldn't police officers normally still be on duty?

"The rumours must be true," Mrs Claus said as she pulled her phone away for the second time, still without an answer from Wiggles and Cornelius. "They probably had spiked eggnogs and are still asleep and hungover."

"So, what do we do now?"

"We call my husband, of course."

For some reason, Father Christmas seemed even more like an authoritative figure than Wiggles and Cornelius. And he certainly wasn't hungover and in bed. He answered Mrs Claus' call almost before the first ring.

In less than half an hour, Father Christmas and Dasher pulled over beside our sleigh.

"Are you both okay?" Father Christmas' concern was evident, and very cute.

"We're fine," Mrs Claus allowed Father Christmas to inspect her arms and legs for any injury.

I thought it was sweet. The two of them were so in love. I hoped their relationship was a glimpse into my future with Nick.

"And you, Holly?" Father Christmas looked at me with worried, loving eyes. I almost melted at the thought of getting in-laws who loved me like their own.

"I'm also fine, Father Christmas," I smiled softly.

"Well, great," he sighed in relief and turned to Mrs Claus. "I came here as soon as you called, dear. What is this about believing Scraper kidnapped Gilbert?"

Mrs Claus turned to me so I'd answer. I said. "Um, I found Gilbert's personalised cookware in Scraper's private stone hut. It's right down the river."

Father Christmas looked over my shoulder towards where the river was. "And you're sure it's his?"

"We are," Mrs Claus confirmed. "It has Gilbert's initials on. We both immediately recognised it."

Father Christmas' eyebrows furrowed together as he paused to think. "It would make sense if Scraper really did take him; the timing of Gilbert's kidnapping, Scraper's anguish about the no prank contract. Maybe he wants to use Gilbert as leverage to negotiate the contract terms."

"Why wouldn't he just say so?" Mrs Claus thought out loud.

"The longer he kept Gilbert, the more desperate we

might become. Hence, we might give in to his demands." Father Christmas concluded.

While the Clauses went back and forth with the logic behind Scraper's motive for Gilbert's kidnapping, I couldn't help but doubt the new clue we had. Maybe my experience as a *detective* had rubbed off on me.

I chimed in. "None of this would explain the black vehicle that Gilbert was last seen riding in. It's not like Scraper has a spare vehicle somewhere around here – the Yule Lads are primitive. They use fireflies as light rather than a gas lamp or electricity."

"Another thing to ponder," Mrs Claus nodded.

"I guess that's true," Father Christmas added. "Maybe that vehicle had nothing to do with Gilbert's kidnapping? Or maybe Scraper had an accomplice back in town."

Mrs Claus put a hand over her mouth. "Oh my, that would be unfortunate. Who would do such a thing?"

"None of this explains Gilbert's note either," I spoke.

"This is giving me a headache," Mrs Claus shook her head. "Nothing seems to be adding up."

"You should rest up and wait for us here," Father Christmas offered.

Mrs Claus firmly disagreed. "I'm seeing Gilbert's disappearance through."

Even I was getting worried. "Stress can cause fatigue, too, Mrs Claus. You can always take a break from this."

"Not when we have all these pieces of clues!" Mrs Claus argued. "The only problem is where in the puzzle they fit... if they even belong in the same puzzle."

"For now, we should deal with this one at a time." Father Christmas said. "I say let's wait for Scraper to appear so we can confront him. We now have evidence against him."

We all climbed into Santa's sleigh – it was one of the

older models – and I was delighted to see that it had its own magic despite its age. The compartment provided us with blankets, camping chairs, a canopy tent, and even flasks of hot tea.

We decided to park the sleighs across the river, where we had a better view of the stone hut. Of course, we made sure we were still hidden within the trees despite our elaborate set-up for the impromptu stakeout.

After we had settled in our seats to wait, Father Christmas began passing out sandwiches from a thermal lunch bag.

Mrs Claus graciously accepted one with an inquisitive tilt of her head. "I don't recall our sleighs providing sandwiches."

"Oh no, they're from Gwen. She saw me heading out and said she had prepared us all a breakfast sandwich." Father Christmas explained.

Mrs Claus groaned. "I should send her away. She's getting too comfortable in Gilbert's kitchen."

"You can do that tomorrow. You can hardly turn her out on Christmas Day." Father Christmas said as he placed his leg over his knee, eyes peeled for any signs of movement on the other side of the river.

I had no idea what to expect from Scraper at this point. This case was indeed baffling. The fact that nothing seemed to align with all the clues suggested we could be looking at a master manipulator.

I wasn't sure Scraper was that – he seemed too angry and too impatient to plan out an entire kidnapping. However, I was hoping Gilbert would also appear once Scraper did.

I had so many questions for Gilbert. Had we really failed to appreciate him? Did he feel unhappy at Claus Cottage?

How long had that been the case and why hadn't he spoken to me?

The three of us watched the stone hut closely for movements. We weren't far from the hut, but an unassuming Yule Lad would easily miss us hiding behind a line of trees.

When we finished our sandwiches and emptied our tea, we finally caught a movement emerging from behind the mountain of boulders across us.

It was Scraper! He was alone, carrying wood in his arms as he approached his stone hut.

I held my breath in case Gilbert might appear behind him, but he didn't.

Where had Scraper been? I wondered. Did he have another hut where he might be keeping Gilbert?

"Stay here," Father Christmas slowly rose out of his chair. "It'll be better if I approach him on my own."

Neither Mrs Claus nor I argued. It was second nature to us that whatever Father Christmas said was generally listened to. He was one of the smartest, most level-headed, and most rational people I knew.

So, I gripped the sides of my seat as Father Christmas jogged down from our camp and effortlessly skated on the rink with just his boots. He let the icy surface take him to the other side.

"Scraper!" I heard Father Christmas bellow.

Scraper paused momentarily, looking around to see who called for him, but Father Christmas was hard to miss. He was a big man with the fitness of a guy in his twenties.

When Scraper spotted him about to climb the riverbank, I thought I saw Scraper's face go pale. Then, he threw all the wood he had and made a run for it.

I gasped, standing up from my seat as I watched Scraper

scramble and climb the rocks in an attempt to get away from Father Christmas.

But Father Christmas had no intention to let Scraper get away; he also climbed the rocks expertly and ran after Scraper in long strides.

"Will he be okay chasing after Scraper alone?" I asked Mrs Claus out of concern.

Mrs Claus watched, slightly at the edge of her seat, but she wasn't as worried as I was. "My husband has great physical strength. He can hold out for a while."

As much as I wanted to cross the river and join the chase, I wondered if I'd only get in the way of Father Christmas, so I just watched him running and jumping rocks from a distance without missing a step.

I was amazed.

After a while, we lost sight of Father Christmas and Scraper; it made me anxious. I wished I could see what was happening.

I held my breath for a moment, waiting for one or both of them to return.

After a few minutes, Father Christmas appeared from behind one of the bigger rocks, but without Scraper.

We waited for him to return to our camp with a disappointed look on his face. "He knows these landscapes better than I do. He slipped through one of those cracks in the mountain and disappeared."

Mrs Claus rubbed a consoling hand on Father Christmas' back. "You did great, sweetheart. But now, do you want me to try calling the police again? If you ask me, Scraper couldn't be any guiltier after taking off like that."

Father Christmas nodded. "Call Wiggles. I think we need a search party over here."

## 17

W ithin the next hour, the search party arrived at the Frozen Flowering Forest.

We had to disrupt Nick's sleep so someone could lead the group back here. As expected, Nick came through for us without a moment's hesitation. His sense of responsibility won over his need to catch up on sleep.

Nick brought Wiggles and Cornelius, both looking a bit worse for wear, with a group of police officers in uniform. Ginger and a few of her regulars from the Polar Arms also arrived. Then there was the sound of whirring blades in the sky and we all gasped as we watched a helicopter approach. It landed carefully on the ground near the frozen river and, to my surprise, out stepped Patrice, her butler, and her pilot.

Father Christmas pulled out maps, radios, and neon-coloured vests to pass around the group of twenty or so people.

"Alright," Father Christmas clapped his hands once to get everyone's attention. "We have reason to believe that one of the Yule Lads, Scraper, had something to do with Gilbert's disappearance. He was last seen around this rocky mountain over an hour ago. Time's already on his side, so we better get moving quickly."

A chorus of agreement echoed among the group.

As Cornelius took charge of assigning the officers to certain locations on the map, Father Christmas led Wiggles into the stone hut for further investigation.

Ginger barked orders at the men who hung on her every word and immediately dispersed with their vests on. Patrice escorted Mrs Claus into the chopper so they could get an aerial view of the place.

Finally, Nick approached me. "Was this why you were sneaking out this morning?"

My eyes widened a little. "You noticed?"

"Well, let's just say my mind is always half-awake."

"Impressive," I smiled, but it slowly faded. I wanted to tell Nick about Slammer visiting me that morning, but I didn't want to get him in trouble. "Mrs Claus and I wanted to keep searching, and we stumbled upon Scraper's stone hut."

I pointed to the abode where Father Christmas was standing outside.

"So, it's definite that Scraper did it then? With the search and all?" Nick inquired.

"Erm... he took off running before we got the chance to question him. But we found Gilbert's bag of cookware inside the hut."

"Looks suspicious enough."

Just then, a guttural roar sent snow and a little bit of icy water whirling into the air as Patrice's chopper whirred to life for take-off. We all turned to watch the metallic beast ascend into the sky; Mrs Claus gave us a little wave from her seat inside.

I waited for the deafening sounds of the engine and the

silver fans to retreat into the distance before I turned to Nick again. But before I could speak to him, a group of twelve Yule Lads – including Slammer, who was feigning innocence – marched towards Nick and me. The older Yule Lad spoke with a raspy voice. "What on earth is happening over here?"

Protective as ever, Nick stepped forward. "My apologies... sir, for disrupting the peace of the forest, but we're looking for Scraper."

"Scraper?"

"What'd he do?"

"Is he in trouble?"

"Are there new laws about stealing pots and pans?"

Those words popped up simultaneously among the Yule Lads.

The older Yule Lad raised his hand, immediately getting the group behind him to settle down. "Why are you looking for him?"

"Is he with you?" I scanned the group, counting only a total of twelve Yule Lads. "Is he, perhaps, at No Carols Cave? We just need to speak with him."

"Speak with him?" The older Yule Lad frowned. "Bringing all these people and sending a chopper in here! You'd only scare him away!"

Nick spoke. "We understand your concern, but we believe Scraper has something to do with our elf's disappearance."

"Ridiculous..." the Yule Lads voice faltered; I could tell the group were loyal to each other but they weren't confident about what Scraper had or hadn't done – Scraper might be guilty.

Instead of pushing Scraper under the bus, the older Yule Lad cleared his throat. "Apart from Scraper, since all of us here signed the contract, isn't it just polite that you respect the forest we live in?"

"What's polite is not kidnapping elves," I couldn't help but blurt. "We've been looking for Gilbert for two days now, and if Scraper is involved in his disappearance, we have the right to know. He's also one of us – much like Scraper is one of you."

A wave of guilt flashed in the Yule Lad's face, and Slammer even looked down on the ground. "Do what you please. Just know that we didn't agree to this... to this hostility! Let's go, boys."

The Yule Lads listened to the older Yule Lad and scampered away from us. Slammer looked back and mouthed the word 'sorry' as he walked with his crutch. I gave him a small nod in response.

With a sigh, I turned to Nick. "We should help in the search. Maybe we'll even find Gilbert without Scraper's help."

Nick took my hand. "Let's go."

The wind howled through the frozen pines as fear gnawed my gut at every climb we made and every stone we turned. Scraper could be hiding in plain sight, using his knowledge of the forest to evade us.

It had been two days since Gilbert went missing, and I was becoming antsy with every passing hour.

Nick and I followed a barely visible trail that snaked up the mountain's side. The air was cold, scented with pine needles and damp earth. Nick and I left little flags on every turn we made. The last thing anyone needed was part of the search party getting lost but the constant sound of Patrice's chopper whirring overhead was reassuring that we'd be found even if we lost our way.

Our silence was only broken by our rasping breaths and the constant crunch of our boots on the icy gravel.

I restlessly scanned the forest floor for any sign – a footstep or a clue. I'd speculate even on a misplaced twig. But this part of the forest remained untouched.

At one point, Nick crouched on the dirt, inspecting what looked like an animal's hooves. "A deer, perhaps?"

I followed the trail the said deer had left; it led straight to the overgrowth, appearing to have snapped plants off their stems as it did so. "It looks like it ran in a hurry."

"The animals here aren't used to seeing people, maybe even Yule Lads. You think Scraper went this way and scared the poor deer?"

"I'm not sure. I don't see any other footsteps."

"Right, we should stick to the trail."

"But what if..." I found myself hoping that maybe it was Gilbert who startled the deer. Maybe he'd even been riding the deer and that's why he left no footprints of his own. At this point, I was willing to entertain any and all possibilities.

Nick placed the small red flag at the beginning of the dense path. "If we don't find anything within the next half hour, promise we'll come back here?"

"Alright," I nodded.

Nick led the way as he used a branch to clear off some of the plants getting in our way. We stayed on course, following the deer tracks. The ever-thickening woods slowly thinned out.

Soon, we were in a small clearing, covered by the dipping crowns of trees, with only a few beams of sunlight seeping in between the spaces of leaves overhead.

There were three deer—a doe and two calves. One of the younger ones was drinking from a small pond, barely a hole in the soil. I looked around, but there were no signs of

Scraper and Gilbert. Still, I called out. "Scraper! Are you here? We just need to talk!"

My voice echoed in the wind but didn't garner a response.

I tried again. "Gilbert!"

Nick simply watched me with worry as he walked around near the trail we followed; he didn't want to startle the deer.

As I watched Nick study the space closer, something fell on my nose and immediately melted. It was a snowflake.

Looking up into the sky, the lone snowflake was followed by more twirling snowflakes, descending into a flurry.

The wind suddenly whipped up with a vengeance. The graceful snowflakes turned into a blizzard, tiny projectiles of snowflakes turning into a relentless horde.

Nick looked up to the little portion of the sky that he could see from all the cowering trees. With a disapproving look on his face, he said to me. "It looks like an incoming snowstorm."

## 18

The search party was immediately called off after the snowstorm began without much of a warning. But back at Candy Cane Hollow, snow barely fell from the sky.

As I looked out the window back at Claus Cottage, most of the search party had gathered in the den while August and Gwen graced us with some hot chocolates.

Mrs Claus had an uncomfortable look on her face as Gwen hopped around the place with an empty tray in her arm... like she was the new Gilbert. But, of course, she would never replace Gilbert.

No one could.

I was the first person to break the silence, still baffled by the snowstorm. "Has the weather in that forest always been so unpredictable?"

Father Christmas replied. "Always. We tried putting weather devices down there, but they all malfunctioned within the first minute. Freak snowstorms, hail, and, at one point, even a *sandstorm* all happened there."

"Wow." I shuddered. "I hate to think Gilbert might be trapped out there in the storm. What do we do next?"

"We have to go back some other time," Father Christmas said, glancing at Mrs Claus who had excused herself and was quietly retreating to their bedroom after another morning of defeat.

Father Christmas saw me watching Mrs Claus, and just as I was about to follow her, he stood up and patted my arm. "I'll go to her, Holly."

The rest of us – Patrice, Wiggles, Cornelius, August, Nick, and I – watched the loving couple disappear.

Wiggles sipped his hot chocolate loudly. "Well, since we found Gilbert's prized possession in Scraper's hut, it's safe to assume he had something to do with the disappearance. We'll process it as evidence for now and bring it back here after examining it."

Nick nodded with understanding. "Thanks, Wiggles. I'm sure Gilbert would appreciate that."

Soon after that, Wiggles and Cornelius left Claus Cottage. As always, *Last Christmas* blared from the Fiat's speakers as they sped off, but even the familiar sound brought no joy to my heart.

Patrice signalled that it was also her time to leave, but before that, she turned to us. "My cousin's going to be alright, right?"

I wished I had confidence in my voice as I tried to reassure her. "We're going to find him, Patrice. We're not giving up."

Patrice nodded, her butler holding the front door open for her. "Well, call me if you need anything – anything at all!"

And I knew she meant that. First were expensive, high-tech drones and then a chopper. If I asked her to look for

Gilbert at the bottom of the ocean, she'd probably have a submarine on standby in her private port.

After we waved goodbye to Patrice, the silence in the room screamed at me. Thankfully, August spoke. "If you found Gilbert's cookware in that Yule Lad's hut, would that mean the letter we found in his bedroom was fake?"

"I don't know what to think anymore," I confessed, vulnerable in the presence of my sister and my fiancé. "There may still be a chance Gilbert took off on his own, but that's a bit harder to believe than anything else."

Nick moved seats so he could sit next to me, then pulled my head over to the space between his neck and shoulder. He smelled like Christmas – like sweet snow, pine, and cinnamon. "You're worrying too much, Holly. Maybe you should rest, just for today. Gilbert's disappearance is taking a toll on us. You and Mum, especially."

"I'm fine," I slowly pulled away from Nick, touching his cheek. "I'll be better when we find Gilbert."

August faked a gagging noise as if she wasn't giddier than I was when I started dating Nick. "Get a room, you two!"

I rolled my eyes at her playfully.

Just then, Gwen came running in from the kitchen with another tray in her hands. This time, with mini donuts. "I baked some pumpkin donut drops! I'm telling you, this is as good as comfort food gets!"

As she set the tray on the coffee table, I was starting to see what Mrs Claus meant by saying that Gwen was getting comfortable in Gilbert's kitchen – she was getting a bit *too* comfortable for a guest.

Gwen acted like she now worked for the Clauses in Gilbert's stead.

Since Mrs Claus was a little drained from our fruitless

searching, I should probably voice our concerns. So, I reached for Gwen's hand on the table. "Gwen, you know we're grateful for all this, right?"

Gwen blinked at me with wide, bright eyes. "I'm doing this because I'm also grateful for all of you. You nursed me back to health, fed me, and even took me to see the sleigh ride in person! It's the least I could do."

I patted the space next to me on the settee, urging Gwen to sit next to me. She reluctantly did, perhaps sensing I was about to tell her something she wouldn't like.

Facing her, I said. "You've already done so much in just two days. More than a *guest* normally would. I guess what I'm saying is if you want to stay here, you should act like a guest... and not our helper elf."

"Are you telling me to leave?" Tears immediately sprung to the bottom of Gwen's eyes.

"No, not at all!" I shrieked, not expecting the professional-looking Gwen to fold to her emotions so quickly. "I just mean you should, erm, take it easy."

Gwen sniffed a bit too dramatically. "It's just that no one has shown me this overwhelming amount of kindness before, and this is my way of showing my appreciation; that's all."

"Of course," I said. Now I felt like the bad guy. "Just don't overwork yourself... is what I'm saying."

"Okay," Gwen wiped her eyes. "I'll be in my room then, like a guest."

Gwen grabbed three pumpkin donut drops before heading upstairs to the guest bedroom.

Nick remarked. "I didn't take her for the emotional type."

"But definitely the bossy type," August shrugged. "She tried to rearrange the cupboards earlier this morning. I stopped her before she could do too much. Gilbert would have lost his mind!"

"I think she's hopeful she could work here," I said. "I'm sure we'll sort that out tomorrow when the office hours at Elf Employment resume. I'll give them a call."

Shaking my head, Nick's face suddenly lit up with an idea. He snapped his fingers. "That's it, Holly!"

August and I turned to him curiously. I said. "What's *it*?"

"Calls!" Nick exclaimed. "We should set up a 24-hour hotline for tips about Gilbert's whereabouts! Surely someone would've seen him. It would make our search easier."

It was a smart idea, but I had one concern. "That's great, Nick, but it's Christmas. Who would operate a 24-hour hotline on a day like this?"

"Santa HQ," Nick answered confidently. "I'm sure Mitzy and her team would be more than willing to do it for us."

"Wouldn't we get in the way of their holiday?"

"Holly, one thing you need to understand about elves is they're dedicated to their jobs. Christmas or not, they're just happy to be of service! We're doing them a favour by giving them something to do."

"Well, you sound certain about that."

"What do you say?" Nick batted his eyelashes at me with expectation. "Should we get that hotline running for Gilbert?"

Seeing Nick's enthusiasm, I felt hope twinkle in my eyes, reflecting his. "You know what, it sounds like a great idea, Nick. Let's do it."

---

## 19

Since Gilbert went missing, all my mornings had been weighed by a heavy amount of dread; it made my stomach churn.

I got out of bed, thinking a cup of something warm would alleviate that psychosomatic stomach pain, but I was almost *not* surprised when I found Gwen humming in the kitchen.

As she heard my footsteps approach the kitchen, Gwen jumped a little, immediately acting like she was caught red-handed. "I... I can explain! It's not what it looks like!"

I glanced at the dining table behind me, where plates filled with eggs Benedict, fruit slices, and a tray of monkey bread were all waiting for the residents of Claus Cottage. I commented. "You weren't making us breakfast?"

"As a guest!" Gwen squeaked, looking around the kitchen frantically before pointing to the sink full of plates. "I wasn't even planning on washing those dishes!"

Although I shouldn't tolerate Gwen and her obvious efforts to take Gilbert's spot, I still felt bad about how she reacted yesterday at the thought of being asked to leave, so I just helped myself to a cup of freshly brewed coffee.

I realised I had barely spoken to Gwen since she had turned up at Claus Cottage, so I figured I should at least get to know her.

I said. "So, Gwen, do you really not have family? There must be a few relatives out there, surely?"

Gwen quietly closed the oven. "No, there's no one. I grew up in an orphanage. But I don't want you to feel sorry for me; that orphanage was every bit like a family while I was there."

I nodded understandingly. "And yet, look how you turned out, you're one of Elf Employment's best elves."

"I worked hard for that title," Gwen beamed proudly.

"I bet you did," I agreed, seeing how hard she was working here. "Was it your idea to be immediately assigned here at Claus Cottage, or did that come automatically with being the best elf in the company?"

"It might as well be automatic. As soon as my superiors heard that the Claus Cottage had a vacancy for an elf position, they assigned me to it right away!"

I cocked my head to one side. "I thought the offices were already closed for Christmas when Gilbert was taken."

Gwen gave a high-pitched giggle. "That's right! But this was an emergency."

"You must've been pretty excited, huh?"

"Who wouldn't be?" Gwen gloated a little. "Frankly, I was more excited about meeting Mrs Claus again."

"Again?" I echoed. "You've seen her out and about in Candy Cane Hollow?"

"Not just that," Gwen explained. "I met her exactly 27 years ago at the orphanage; I was eight years old when she walked into the building on a Christmas morning. She brought toys and candies and clothes for all the children—for all of us. I remembered thinking I wanted to get to know her."

Gwen smiled at the memory, continuing. "She said I had a beautiful name and she gave me a stuffed reindeer. I still have it back at my apartment."

I could feel the warmth emanating from Gwen; her slight desperation to work here was finally making sense. She had felt a connection with Mrs Claus that day. Surely, when she heard there was an opening at the Claus Cottage, she had come here quickly, having waited for this opportunity all her life.

I smiled at her recollection. "Well, isn't that sweet? Have you told Mrs Claus? It might make her feel better."

"Oh, I wouldn't impose..." Gwen's smile slowly faded. "I admit I was a little upset she didn't recognise me when I first came here. It must be the glasses and the haircut."

"Don't take it personally, I don't even remember everyone I met 27 days ago," I remarked.

"Oh, no, Holly. We didn't just meet 27 years ago; we also met five years ago at an art exhibit."

"You did?"

"I'll always remember since she helped me that day," Gwen narrated. "I was a new employee at Elf Employment and I was assigned to work at an art exhibit. I was still clumsy then. The curator pulled me aside and gave me an earful for poorly hanging an exquisite painting. I was near tears as she scolded me, you know? But just like a guardian angel, Mrs Claus walked in and told the curator to take it easy on me."

Gwen sighed and swooned.

I couldn't help but relate to her – Mrs Claus also walked

up to me like an angel after my little car accident that brought me to Candy Cane Hollow.

"Mrs Claus probably doesn't even know she inspired you, huh?" I smiled.

"She doesn't have to know; I'm just glad to be around her," Gwen replied.

"And you're always welcome here, you know that, right? As long as you don't try and take Gilbert's spot." I quipped.

Gwen's face turned crimson in shame. "But Holly, you can't possibly manage here without a house elf much longer. If Gilbert isn't home soon, you'll have to allow me to begin work. It's in the agreement."

I gazed at the floor as I considered Gwen's words. As much as I wanted to argue, she had a point. Claus Cottage couldn't continue indefinitely without a house elf. Unless we found Gilbert, and soon, we would have to make the awful decision to accept he wasn't returning. My stomach churned at the idea of such a thing.

"But for now, I'm just a guest! I... I know! In fact, *you* should gather everyone for breakfast! If you don't mind..."

"Sure, Gwen. No problem," I said, secretly glad to end the conversation.

I went around the house, knocking on the bedroom doors. I started with Nick, who gave me a long, sleepy hug as he sat up from his bed. Then, August and Tom's bedroom, where Jeb was just getting dressed in a pair of cute snowman-themed pyjamas. Finally, Father Christmas and Mrs Claus' bedroom.

Father Christmas opened the door, stepped out into the hall, and closed the door behind him. He said. "Mrs Claus isn't doing so well this morning. I think it's best if she rests."

"She's not?" Nick's voice echoed behind me.

I turned around just in time to see Nick's face drain of

colour. "What's wrong with her? Maybe Holly should look at her."

"It's just one of those fevers," Father Christmas explained. "She'd feel worse if she troubled all of you, don't you think?"

"But dad..."

"I heard you're running a hotline for Gilbert," Father Christmas expertly changed the subject. "Have you heard anything from Mitzy?"

Nick opened and closed his mouth before finally answering. "Holly and I will visit Santa HQ later today to check on that."

*We will?* I wondered with excitement. I was glad to have a job to do.

"And Holly," Father Christmas called my attention. "Aren't you opening your surgery today? I bet there are patients who'd love to see you."

"I am," I answered. "Although I sent out a notice, I'll only be working mornings so I can still help look for Gilbert."

"Thank you. I wouldn't want you to set aside your job while everything else is happening. Your work is valuable."

"Thank you, Father Christmas," I smiled. "Um, the table is set for breakfast. Would you like me to prepare a tray for Mrs Claus?"

"I'll do it," Father Christmas offered, pointing us down the hall so we could all head together to the dining room.

We did, and we found August, Tom, and Jeb already waiting for us. Gwen sat confidently at the table as if she hadn't just prepared the meal. However, Father Christmas didn't join us; he chose to eat with Mrs Claus in their bedroom, which I thought was really sweet – he didn't want his wife to eat alone.

We all sat in comfortable silence as we ate.

Gwen might have been firm about not doing the dishes, but she kept glancing at the kitchen as she ate with us. In the end, August did the dishes while Gwen passed her things item by item. It clearly pained her not to just do the job herself.

Nick and I drove together to the High Street, where my surgery had quite the line outside.

Father Christmas was right – I couldn't neglect my job.

I kissed Nick on the cheek, thankful that we used a car on this semi-sunny day, or the crowd would erupt in giddiness if they saw me kiss Nick.

As soon as I hopped out of the car, the people outside immediately greeted me, and I greeted them back. Inside, my secretary smiled at me sadly. "I heard about Gilbert..."

"Don't worry about it; we'll find him," I assured her – I assured *me*.

I put on my white gown and got to work immediately.

I only had four hours to get through all my scheduled patients for the morning, so I intended to put all my attention to my work as the local GP.

Believe me when I say I tried my best to focus, but almost all of my patients brought me gifts to comfort me after having heard about Gilbert's disappearance. It was an endless morning of apologies and assurances and sweet treats.

Still, I appreciated each one of them.

That morning, I treated stomach pain from a gluttonous night of binge-eating, a second-degree burn from a small cooking accident, and four separate cases of cranberries stuck up noses.

At exactly three minutes after noon, I finished checking all my patients for the day. I asked my secretary to close up because Nick was already waiting for me outside.

I ran towards his car so we could head to Santa HQ and check the hotline for any progress.

When we got there, the sound of ringing phones and conversations overlapped.

The production floor had been cleared to make room for rows and rows of tables with notepads and telephones and about fifty elves working behind them.

"Wow," I didn't hide my amazement. "You pulled this off in just one day?"

"Mitzy did all the work," Nick said, giving credit where it was due. "Now, where is she?"

As if Mitzy could sense Nick was looking for her, she popped her head from under one of the far tables. "Santa!"

Mitzy hurried towards Nick and me. She gave me a small nod. "Holly."

"Mitzy. Are you okay?" I nodded back.

She glanced back at the desk with a flippant wave of her hand. "Just wired up the last computer. We're all set."

"Any new clues about Gilbert?" Nick asked Mitzy.

Mitzy swiftly turned to her clipboard and flipped through four or five pages before handing it to Nick. "We've had all kinds of calls all day; everyone's saying they saw Gilbert all over town!"

Nick also flipped through the clipboard where Mitzy had put down the calls – none of them led them to Gilbert.

"Who's checking all these calls?" I inquired.

"I have a team of elves responding to all the locations," Mitzy answered proudly. "But at this rate of phone calls, we might need to ask the police to collaborate with us."

"I'm sure Wiggles would be happy to help," I replied. "We'll call him to send a few police officers down here."

Mitzy nodded. "Great! I hope you don't mind me saying this, Santa, but we've been here since yesterday, and we haven't found a real clue about Gilbert yet. I'm starting to think he's really at that mystical forest with that menacing Yule Lad!"

Nick sighed as he returned Mitzy's clipboard. "Well, that's still a possibility."

"Are you going to look for him again?"

"We could check if the weather there has improved, then we will."

"If you are, I might have a piece of advice," Mitzy looked at us with anticipation. "I've been reading about Yule Lads, and I figured they know Scraper and the forest better than anyone, so you should get them to search for you."

"How?" Even I was intrigued.

"With bribes! Yule Lads are easy to please! So, I prepared a few things you could bring to butter them up." Mitzy snapped her fingers, and a group of elves ran up behind her with a bulky Santa sack.

Mitzy explained. "I have twelve premium items for those twelve Yule Lads who aren't on the run – there's meat, candy, cake, silver spoons, doorknobs, and even a cow for fresh milk. I labeled it all so you won't get confused about who it belongs to."

"You placed a *live* cow inside that sack?" I exclaimed with worry.

"Of course not, silly!" Mitzy laughed. "The cow is outside, ready to be taken to the forest."

Nick's mouth was wide open, impressed by his best elf employee. "How did you even think of all of this?"

"It's my job to make your life easier," she slid the sack towards Nick's feet. "Now, off you go. We are fine here."

"Thank you, Mitzy," Nick said with sincerity.

As we exited Santa HQ with newfound confidence,

Mitzy ran after us, this time with a scroll in her hand. "Santa, wait! I almost forgot."

Two elves helped Nick load the sack into a spare sleigh they had at the HQ basement parking.

Nick turned around to meet Mitzy. "What is it?"

"Father Christmas came over here yesterday and wanted me to rework the contract into something the Yule Lads couldn't resist," Mitzy handed the scroll. "Like I said, I've been studying the Yule Lads, and I think I just came up with the most perfect contract they couldn't say no to."

Nick accepted the scroll and unrolled it so we could read it.

As I skimmed through the clauses, my eyes widened – this contract would definitely butter them right up even without our 'gifts.'

Way to go, Mitzy.

## 20

"We come bearing gifts..." Nick said awkwardly as he stood at the mouth of No Carols Cave.

Thankfully, the weather had returned to icy and sunny and the snow had stopped falling.

Only Slammer stood before us, anxiously glancing over his shoulder. "They're, um, requesting that you leave the forest. They don't want to deal with any of you right now."

I tried to hide my disappointment as I glanced at Nick before replying. "We came all this way to put an end to this feud."

Which wasn't exactly a lie.

Nick and I agreed that we would ultimately find a middle ground after we got the Yule Lads to get Scraper to talk to us. Maybe find Gilbert. After all, if Scraper kidnapped Gilbert to regain their life and purpose, they now would with this new contract.

Scraper lowered his voice to a half-whisper. "Frankly, they were willing to help until you allowed a bunch of outsiders into the forest. One of the reasons why we agreed to the contract thirty years ago was because we liked our peace and privacy. You could say the search party was intrusive."

"We're desperate out here," Nick confessed. "It's been three days since Gilbert went missing. Surely you can understand."

A part of me wanted to pinpoint that it was Slammer who brought us here, but I didn't want to mess with the balance of the universe. There's a saying to not shoot the messenger – right now, Slammer was just a messenger for the rest of the group.

Slammer looked genuinely conflicted; I knew he wanted to help us, too, but we were within earshot of the other Yule Lads. Instead, I used that to my advantage.

Recalling what Mitzy said about Yule Lads being easy to please, I made my voice louder as I crouched to check the items in the sack. "We brought a bunch of things over here as a peace offering. We have a cow for milk, a potted yew tree, gourmet sausages, and high-quality beef. Oh, we even have a silver spoon and a platinum doorknob, too!"

At that point, I could see a few Yule Lads peeking from the rocky walls of the cave, so I continued. "We have a painting of a window, a box of whipped cream, and, oh, candies and chocolates!"

With those tempting details, five or six Yule Lads had completely stepped out of the shadows, peering over Slammer's shoulders.

One after another, they took hesitant steps closer towards the bulging sack; their eyes lingered on the names taped to each item.

"Is this mine?" Peeper asked as he pointed to the painting of a window, complete with an enchanting scene of a lavender farm.

I nodded as I handed it to him. "It is – take it."

Peeper hesitated, but after a few seconds, he quickly grabbed it and rushed back to the depths of the cave, giggling with excitement.

For a moment, the other Yule Lads stood perfectly still, as if waiting for *something* to happen to Peeper as soon as he got inside the cave, but when nothing did, the other Yule Lads grabbed their gifts.

Even Slammer couldn't resist his platinum doorknob, testing the weight in his hands.

After ten Yule Lads had been enticed to collect their gift, only the potted yew tree was left – it was for the oldest Yule Lad, Clod.

How impolite of me to not have learned his name earlier.

The commotion had made him step out of the cave with a disappointed gaze. "If I planted my own yew tree, it would take the fun out of sucking other people's yews. Did you consider that before coming here with bribes?"

"It's not a…" I stopped myself, knowing full well it was a bribe more than a peace offering. So, I just decided to be honest. "I mean, it is a bribe, but we only brought it here so you would help us find Gilbert. That's all we're asking for."

Clod walked closer to the yew tree, gently touching the yellow fruits. "Of course you are, until you decide you want something else as well."

He turned to Slammer and gave him a dismissive nod, and Slammer seemed to act on that by returning inside the cave.

Since Clod was the oldest, I guessed that he was the most respected among the group. If we got him to say yes, it would be a done deal from there hopefully. He turned to us once more. "Do you want us to help you arrest Scraper? Is that it?"

"No," Nick spoke. "As you can see, it's just Holly and me this time. We just want to talk to him. If he really doesn't have Gilbert, wouldn't he want to clear his name?"

"But you think he has Gilbert."

"Only because he ran away from us before we got to ask him questions."

"Maybe you scared him into running."

"Maybe he was afraid of something else, so he ran."

To our surprise, Clod let out a hearty laughter. "Oh, how you've grown up, Nick Claus."

That laughter made me loosen up. *Phew.*

As I turned to Nick, he was also caught off guard, but the crease on his eyebrows relaxed. "You brought me here when I was a child, didn't you?"

"Do you remember now?" Clod said, a smile forming on his face.

"I always thought it was a dream, but I guess I do." Nick paused. "And if there's anything I remember clearly, it's that you were good to me. So, I'd like to think none of you would hurt Gilbert. Not even Scraper."

I didn't expect Nick's vulnerability to be the better bribe, but Clod picked up the potted plant and rocked it in his arms like a precious baby. "Come in; we have a fire raging inside."

Seeing the relief on Nick's face, I reached for his hand. "You did a great job, Nick."

Nick kissed the back of my hand.

We followed Clod into the cave, where the eleven Yule Lads were all enjoying their new gifts. The big black cat rolled on its belly as it welcomed us; Nick watched it with a peculiar expression.

"He's harmless," I told Nick as I touched his fur, instantly burying my hand in inches of it.

"I remember him," Nick said with a smile. It was clear he had no memory of the cat until seeing it just now, and the childlike excitement on his face was a joy to see. The whole Claus family were cat lovers.

Two Yule Lads brought us wooden chairs to sit on, and so we did, grateful for their hospitality.

Clod set aside his plant and then started the conversation. "So, you want us to help you find Scraper so you can talk to him?"

I nodded. "We figured you know the forest better – you know Scraper better! The odds of you finding him and convincing him to talk to us are high. We just need to know where Gilbert is."

Clod sighed. "We do believe that Scraper might've had some involvement with Gilbert's disappearance, but I want to assure you that if he has him, he wouldn't hurt him. I'm sure he's only holding onto him to get Father Christmas to fold."

"No need," Nick answered, pulling out the scroll contract from his inner jacket. "Here, we came up with a contract. Scraper wants to stay true to his life purpose, right? It's all here – an exclusive day for Yule Lads to get out into the city and play *harmless* tricks to their heart's desires."

Looking around, the Yule Lads nodded and muttered in agreement. This was a good sign.

Clod took the scroll, unrolled it, and read the new contract. After a while, he said. "April 1..."

"Yes," Nick answered confidently. "Pulling pranks at Christmastime is quite a hassle for the people of Candy Cane Hollow, don't you think? You wouldn't like it if we came in here and ruined your Christmas by stealing a few things here and there, would you?"

Clod nodded slowly. "You're right."

"So?" I watched Clod, hopefully.

Clod took a second to look around at all the Yule Lads. I held my breath as he spoke. "Boys, we're heading to the forest. Slammer, stay here and watch the guests. Make sure they don't steal... rocks."

Laughter erupted in the room; even Nick and I laughed, but mostly with relief.

## 21

S lammer had hummed the same song almost a hundred times – at least, that was what it felt like since I'd lost count at some point.

But in the silence of the cave, apart from the wind blowing from the cave's mouth and the fire cackling before us, there wasn't anything to listen to, so it was Slammer humming as he cleaned the cave.

About two hours later, we could finally hear the sound of incoming chatter. I turned to Nick, who stood up from his seat, waiting for the Yule Lads to appear at the entrance.

"Come on now, Scraper," Clod's voice bounced around the cave walls.

When Slammer heard Scraper's name, he scrambled on his legs and climbed the ladder leading to his bedroom, with impressive speed given his injury. He closed the door behind him, his new platinum doorknob glinting at the fire's light.

Clod was the first Yule Lad to enter; behind him was Scraper. *Finally.*

Scraper looked a little bit out of sorts – dirt on his face, grime on his long beard, soil under his nails, and maybe he was even a bit paler and thinner.

"Are you okay, Scraper?" That was the first thing I said as I saw him. It was hard to switch off my medical instincts, even when faced with Gilbert's possible kidnapper.

Scraper scoffed, looking elsewhere.

Clod turned to the other Yule Lads. "Head inside your rooms, boys. Let's give them some privacy. Go on, now."

While the group groaned, they still listened to Clod's command. They stomped and trudged their way into their own cave bedrooms, clearly unhappy to be missing out on whatever unfolded next. I was sure they were all listening through their wooden doors anyway. The acoustics in the cave travelled.

Clod cleared his throat, pointing his thumb back to the entrance. "I'll be sitting outside in case Scraper tries to run again."

With a snap of a finger, the black cat followed Clod outside. I supposed Scraper could outrun Clod, but not that long-limbed cat.

The silence among us was uncomfortable and I almost wished for Slammer's humming again.

Nick broke the silence. "Sit with us, Scraper. We just want to talk. We promise."

Stubborn, Scraper crossed his arms over his chest and leaned on the wall instead. "Please, as if you didn't have the entirety of Candy Cane Hollow looking to arrest me."

"We weren't trying to arrest you last time," I explained. "It's true that we called Candy Cane Custody, but only so they could help us look for you after you ran away from Father Christmas."

"Well, he's one intimidating man," Scraper huffed.

"That's why you ran?" Nick asked.

"I ran because he was chasing me."

"But he wasn't," I said, having seen it all from across the Rink River. "He wasn't even running towards you; you bolted the moment you saw him."

"Because he was out to get me!" Scraper took a deep breath before speaking in his normal and gruff tone. "I bet Father Christmas was out here for revenge because I didn't sign the contract. That's it, isn't it? Unbelievable."

Nick frowned. I didn't think I had ever seen him look so serious. "I don't appreciate you speaking ill of my father, Scraper. He is not a spiteful man; you should know that better than anyone. Even after you took his son –"

"After we took you, he banished us! He kept us in here!"

"No, he kept you from goofing off around town. That's not banishment. You've always been welcome to come and go into Candy Cane Hollow as you pleased."

"Huh! Sure, I can imagine the welcome we'd get!"

"Enough," I interjected strongly. "Whatever happened in the last thirty years, it's over now. We're here to make amends. You must've heard about the new contract, right? That's why you returned."

Scraper glared at me, but I could tell from his quivering irises that I was right – he was here for the contract. "I would be selfish if I put my brothers in the middle of this senseless war. All I wanted was to get us back our purpose."

Nick handed the scroll to Scraper. "Here it is. Do the honours and be the first Yule Lad to sign it."

Scraper just stared at the contract, his hopes within a fingertip's touch, yet he couldn't bring himself to take it.

I tapped Nick's arm, and he handed the scroll to me. I walked closer to Scraper and placed the scroll in his hands. "Read it. If you don't like it, we'll change it. We'll keep revising this contract until it works for everyone."

Scraper's hand gripped around the scroll a little too tight. "Why are you doing this?"

"Because we want to turn over a new leaf," I answered with sincerity. "You probably carried this existential crisis for way too long, and now, we want to help you."

*Then you can help us.* I withheld that part for now.

I stepped backward and gave Scraper some space to go through the contract.

Nick and I watched him unroll the scroll and meticulously read through every line of the new contract Mitzy had worked so hard on. I silently decided to give her a proper thank you when we returned to Candy Cane Hollow.

When Scraper got to the end of the contract, I saw his back heave and fall with a deep exhale. He finally spoke. "So, you'll preserve the forest's sanctity, give us a day to fool around town, and even provide us with a lifetime supply of food that isn't available here in the forest?"

I glanced at Nick so he would answer. Nick nodded. "Anything you need – I'm sure this forest doesn't have peppermint bark candies, right?"

Was I sensing agreement between them? For some reason, Scraper seemed like he was slowly lowering his defences.

Scraper glanced back at the scroll.

I wished I could read his mind.

With a nod, Scraper offered his open hand. "You got a pen?"

I felt my insides melt with relief as soon as Scraper said that. Confetti popped into my head.

And it wasn't just me who rejoiced.

All of a sudden, all the doors on the caves above us opened simultaneously – Yule Lads cheered as they hurried down, most of them with a pen to offer to Scraper. I was right that they were listening to our conversation the entire time!

The cave erupted with joyous cheers as Scraper signed the contract.

The Yule Lads then passed the scroll around so they could all sign. Clod entered the cave again laughing, pleased by what he was looking at. "I'm glad we can put all of this behind us."

Slammer was the last of the group to sign the scroll, so he limped it across to Clod. "All we need is your signature, and it's official."

"Well, don't mind if I do," Clod said with a hearty chuckle.

I watched closely as the pen point landed on the grainy page of the yellowish paper. Every stroke Clod made felt magical. And as soon as he had finished signing his name with an unexpected flourish, I kept waiting for the scroll to light up or burst into flames or something ceremonious, but nothing like that happened.

Still, everyone in the room clapped and hollered.

This moment was so beautiful – like two countries signing a peace pact – I almost forgot the more important thing.

As the happy noise died down, Nick turned to Scraper with a smile and an expectation. "So, Scraper, would you lead us to Gilbert now?"

Scraper looked at Nick, unblinking. "What do you mean?"

Thrown off, I stammered. "You... you were supposed to return Gilbert to us since we revised the contract as you wanted. Remember?"

"Who on Candy Cane Hollow is Gilbert?" Scraper replied, his voice laced with puzzlement.

How could he not know? How could he forget our previous conversation at Claus Cottage? Was he feigning innocence?

I glanced at Clod, who shrugged his shoulders at me in equal confusion. Slammer avoided eye contact with me. Everyone else waited for Scraper to do something – maybe laugh and say he was just kidding. But nothing.

What Scraper said a while back suddenly hit me like an ice block. Scraper ran away because he thought Father Christmas was coming for him because he had not signed the contract! He didn't run away because he had Gilbert.

Scraper didn't have Gilbert.

Perhaps Nick could see the colour in my face drain; he held me by the elbow to support me. "Are you okay, Holly?"

I gazed at Nick through glassy eyes. "I don't understand. If Scraper didn't take him, where is he?"

Nick turned to Scraper once more. "Are you saying you really didn't take Gilbert?"

"Oh! You mean your missing elf?" Scraper clarified. "I already told you back at your house, I didn't take him. What made you think I did?"

It was no time to point fingers – I was to blame, too. I wanted somebody to be responsible for Gilbert's disappearance. I knew Slammer and the Yule Lads meant well when they thought Scraper had him, too.

But Scraper's innocence was evident in his face and voice.

I could see that clearly now.

I heard Nick reply. "We found Gilbert's pots and pans in your hut, Scraper. It was a very special set for Gilbert."

"But I steal pots and pans; that's what I was made for," Scraper responded matter-of-factly.

"I know, but this cookware was hidden under Gilbert's

bed, and he sometimes even slept with it. How could you have found it?"

"I'm not sure I follow."

I chimed in. "It was a set of enamel iron cast cookware inside a navy blue carry-on bag."

"Ah!" Scraper's face brightened in recognition. "The one with the letters on the handles?"

"Yes," I breathed, although it was shallow.

"I found that outside Claus Cottage's driveway," Scraper said. "It was discarded right by the entrance. I figured it was thrown away, so I took it home."

I didn't think my heart could sink further into my stomach until now. It was like a black hole of grief had opened up under my skin.

How could Gilbert's most precious cookware be discarded at the cottage's driveway? If that were true, how could we have missed it?

The better question was – did someone leave it there? Did Gilbert?

## 22

"I just don't understand," my heartbreak seeped into every syllable I uttered. I stared at the bag of cookware Wiggles and Cornelius had just dropped off here at Santa HQ. "Why would Gilbert leave his precious cookware?"

Nick let out a defeated sigh – apart from getting the Yule Lads back in our good graces, we hadn't accomplished anything regarding Gilbert. "I wish I had the answer, too, Holly. I'm starting to think Gilbert might have…"

I held my breath as Nick struggled to say the words I dreaded out loud.

"Never mind," Nick shook his head as if it would shift his mind from such thoughts. "What did Wiggles say about the cookware? Were they able to lift off prints?"

"Only Scraper's," I informed him.

"Just Scraper's? Not even Gilbert's?"

"I know, which makes me think that whoever dropped it off must've wiped it clean."

Of course, it wasn't unlike Gilbert to wipe things clean but even I was surprised that his cleanliness reached such high standards. I still refused to believe Gilbert had left voluntarily and without these; they were his prized possessions.

Or was I too emotional about this case? Should I just leave it up to Wiggles and Cornelius?

The silence between Nick and me blanketed the room, somehow uncomfortable despite our familiarity. But only because we were holding back from saying things that could hurt us.

My gaze lingered on the picture window behind Nick's desk, the sight of a nearby reindeer farm took my mind off Gilbert for a few seconds. The herd of reindeer grazed the snowy landscape and jumped through hurdles.

I wished I could allow myself to get lost in the tranquil scene. At least for those animals, life was continuing as normal.

"Oh," I squeaked. "What did Mitzy say about the hotline? Any new calls?"

"She said she'll just finish her end-of-the-day report and come over here to discuss it with us," Nick said.

"Isn't she just a darling?"

"She is. No wonder dad insisted I keep her around even after he retired."

"Mitzy did save us back there with the Yule Lads."

"I supposed an elf would know other elves better."

I nodded with a smile I plastered for the sake of the lighthearted conversation. "It'd be nice to talk like this again, huh?"

Nick rose from his red velvet executive chair and spread his arms open. "Come here, Holly."

I glanced up at him. "I thought you don't condone inappropriate workplace behaviour?"

"I make exceptions, especially if it's for my fiancée. Now, come on. Don't embarrass me."

I chuckled at the sight of Santa Claus opening his muscular arms for me as comfort. Still, I stood up from my seat and melted into his chest and felt his strong arms around me. "This feels nice."

"Well, I don't mind staying like this for a while," Nick swayed in place with me. And I just let him.

I didn't realise how much I needed this until I was finally enveloped in Nick's arms.

My chest welled up with emotions the longer I buried my face in Nick's sweater. He smelled of cocoa, cloves and pine. Even the soft thread his jumper was made from brought me a sense of calm.

It was hard not to drown in the ocean of emotions I had been swimming in for the last few days – fear, disappointment, and grief grappled at my ankles like an anchor.

"Do you feel any better now?" Nick muttered in my hair.

"I do, thank you," I replied, pulling away to give Nick a quick peck on the lips.

"Now *I* feel better," Nick grinned.

With perfect timing, a quiet rap on the door forced Nick and I to move a decent distance from each other; we might be engaged, but this was still his workplace.

Nick returned to his seat behind the big desk. "Come on in."

I also sat back in my chair when the oak door opened. "Sorry for the slight delay. I had to make copies of this afternoon's agenda for us."

Mitzy walked in with three identical clipboards in her arms; she handed us one each. "You'll find a detailed and comprehensive file of all the phone calls we received in the last 24 hours."

The thirty-page thick document baffled me. "Wow, Mitzy, you really outdid yourself."

"Oh, don't be silly," Mitzy said as she sat on the chair opposite me. "This is just regular paperwork for me."

I glanced at Nick, who nodded proudly. "You should've seen her presentations on the night before Christmas."

"Anyway," Mitzy spoke with authority. "If you turn to page three, you'll see a summary that I prepared based on all these 875 phone calls."

I followed her direction and turned my file to page three – a colourful pie graph in Christmas colours was labelled with numbers and words. This really seemed like an executive meeting and I was touched by how seriously Mitzy was taking the project.

Mitzy explained. "A whopping 61% were prank calls – mostly from teenagers who thought it'd be funny to say that every elf with a green suit on is Gilbert. Persistent, if you ask me. Then 29% are from people who'd like to wish Santa a Merry Christmas. Just 4% were phone calls we followed up on, from an elf sleeping in a parking lot to an elf walking around town disguised as a Christmas tree – none of them were Gilbert. Believe it or not, 3% were wrong numbers, and the last 3% were disconnected."

"As always, Mitzy, this is… extraordinary." Nick praised her. "But you said only 4% of these calls deserved a follow-up?"

"That's exactly 35 elves we checked up on – two of them were called in at least three times each. To be fair, they did look like Gilbert."

I couldn't help but frown. "Thirty-five out of 875 calls would suggest our hotline's not exactly… effective."

Nick's eyebrows furrowed as he looked at these figures closely. "It sounded like a great idea yesterday."

"It is!" I quickly clarified. "I'm just saying that it seems clear now that nobody has seen Gilbert. Which makes one wonder…"

I paused – there I was again, struggling with statements that shed doubt on Gilbert.

"…if Gilbert left on his own." Mitzy finished my sentence for me. "I mean, it's a possibility. Maybe Gilbert's having a quarter-life crisis. Who knows?"

*We* would know – especially Mrs Claus. Something like a quarter-life crisis would be hard to miss when you live under the same roof.

But if we missed Gilbert's cookware sitting out in the driveway, what else could we have missed?

Was I giving myself too much credit when I might've been a lousy housemate to Gilbert?

All these thoughts had me constantly doubting myself, too. I had to get out of this headspace soon or I would be no help to anyone.

"What if he really did?" Nick finally said it out loud, trying to be logical rather than emotional about it. "He voluntarily got into that black vehicle on his own. He left a note in his handwriting, and abandoned his favourite thing. It's hard not to think that he didn't… run away."

I heard my voice thicken with emotion. "Are you suggesting we give up?"

Nick looked at me with sad eyes. "The black cars were a dead end. Even our only suspect, Scraper, led us nowhere. We've been running around chasing our tails for three days."

"Maybe we're looking at his disappearance from the wrong angle," I argued weakly, knowing I had nothing more to add.

But Mitzy did.

"Hmm," she paused. "Maybe Holly's right – what if there's a piece of evidence you looked at in the wrong way and that completely threw off your investigation? Kidnappers these days have become smart. Perhaps they intended to throw you off."

"But what evidence?" Nick considered this.

The whisper of an idea buzzed in my head. "I…"

Nick and Mitzy both looked at me eagerly.

"Go on, Holly. What is it?" Nick encouraged.

I took a deep breath. "I guess… Ethan has been acting strange."

Mitzy frowned. "Ethan Evergreen?"

I nodded. "You know him?"

"I don't like to gossip."

"Please, Mitzy. If you know anything at all, now isn't the time to be shy," Nick said.

Mitzy nodded, as if his word was a direct order. "It's just… there are rumours around town. Evergreen Emporium is in trouble and he's been asking strange questions. I think the pressure is getting to him."

"What kind of strange questions?"

Mitzi's cheeks flushed. "It's nonsense, really. He's been asking about hidden treasure."

"Hidden treasure?" I repeated, and the words sparked a memory. Where had I heard something similar recently?

Mitzy gave an awkward laugh. "Nonsense, right? Stress can do strange things to a person. I just hope things get better for him. That store has been in his family for years."

We all sat with our thoughts momentarily.

Then, Mitzy said. "Among all of this, the oddest evidence to me seems like the note. What if Gilbert didn't write it?"

"But the handwriting..." I replied, recalling the scene when I first saw it. "Mrs Claus confirmed Gilbert wrote it."

"Elves' handwriting is often similar," Mitzy explained. "Probably because most of us went to the same elf academy to get our certifications."

I let out a half-gasp that sounded like I was trying to catch my breath.

Two pairs of eyes turned to me questioningly. Nick said. "What is it, Holly?"

My mouth ran dry, and my heartbeat quickened as I answered. "I think I know what we missed – no, I think I know who took Gilbert."

## 23

B y the time we got home to Claus Cottage, I was ninety percent sure I finally knew who had taken Gilbert.

When we walked into the den, snow piled and melted on my shoulders; everyone was waiting for us.

Father Christmas' arm was around Mrs Claus' shoulders. Gwen tried not to grab the tray of cookies from August's arms as she also carried Jeb in a body carrier – acting like the guest she was. Tom followed after August with mugs of hot chocolate. Wiggles and Cornelius were the first ones to grab hot chocolates. Patrice stood off to herself in the corner of the room, anxiously biting her nails.

And, there, sitting perfectly straight-backed by the fire, was Ethan Evergreen.

"You're both back," Mrs Claus spoke with a faint rasp in her voice. "Now, why did you call all of us here?"

Nick immediately approached Mrs Claus' side and whispered. "Are you feeling better now, Mum?"

Mrs Claus nodded weakly at Nick, keeping her eyes

glued to me. I spoke. "Thank you all for gathering here despite the short notice."

I nodded at Wiggles and Cornelius. "As you all know, we have been working tirelessly trying to find Gilbert. And it had come to a point where we even started believing that, perhaps, our loyal elf took off on his own."

My eyes darted from across the room, everyone listening to every word I said. "Except Gilbert didn't do that."

Mrs Claus' back straightened as I said that, her senses magnified, ready to jump into action if I said so.

I continued. "It has taken us over 72 hours, almost tearing the universe's very fabric apart by taking our chances with the Yule Lads, a couple of drones, a helicopter, a search party, a snowstorm, and more. All these led us to this moment, and to Gilbert's kidnapper."

"What are you trying to say, dear?" Mrs Claus inquired hopefully.

"I'm saying that Gilbert's kidnapper has been among us, all this time." Saying it out loud came with a bittersweet aftertaste in my mouth. An indirect admission that we had been fooled from the very start. But if we hadn't, I wouldn't have ultimately realised we were being duped.

The room suddenly fell quiet as if waiting for the kidnapper to reveal himself. Even Wiggles and Cornelius pointed at each other questioningly. Ethan gazed into the fire as if hypnotised.

"Who is it?" Mrs Claus asked bravely; betrayal couldn't deter her desire to find Gilbert.

"It's been a real puzzle to work that out. The Yule Lads kept us so busy and focused on them. It meant we didn't see things that were right under our roof. Like you, Ethan."

"Me?" His voice quivered.

"You've been hanging around here, far too interested in

Gilbert's disappearance. You even broke a window trying to get in here, didn't you?"

"I only wanted to help," Ethan stammered.

"That's commendable. Especially with your store facing such hard times."

To my surprise, he began to cry. "Oh, Holly, I don't know what I'll do if I can't save the business. My parents poured their hearts into it and here I am, ruining it all."

"You believed Gilbert could help you save the store, right?"

He shook his head. "I don't know what you mean. Gilbert was my friend."

"Was?" Mrs Claus repeated, her voice barely a whisper.

"You wanted him to lead you to the treasure," I continued.

Ethan laughed. "That's ridiculous. There's no such thing as treasure!"

"In Claus Cottage, where snowflakes gleam, A hidden treasure, like a dream," I began to recite.

"Oh, Ethan!" Mrs Claus exclaimed, her hand flying to her mouth.

"That's just a silly poem," Ethan said.

"Perhaps. But for a person as desperate to save their store as you are, it could be just the thing to save you. You knew that Gilbert would never reveal any secrets about Claus Cottage willingly, so you plotted to kidnap him."

Ethan began to wail. "I would never have hurt him, you have to believe me! I just wanted... I needed to try everything!"

"But Ethan, the treasure in Claus Cottage isn't material. It's love. If you had just come to us, dear, we could have helped," Mrs Claus said, her own voice full of emotion.

"You wrote the note and hid it in Gilbert's room," I said.

Ethan nodded. "But I... oh, I can't bear it! I can't even kidnap someone right! And now Gilbert's dead, and it's all because of me!"

There was a heavy silence for a moment as his words sank in across the room.

"Gilbert's dead?" Father Christmas asked, his booming voice even louder than usual.

"You killed our Gilbert?" August asked, rising from her seat.

"What? No! I..."

"You said you wouldn't have hurt him," Nick said.

"And I wouldn't! I never even got the chance! I..."

"What do you mean?" August asked.

"He means that he didn't kidnap Gilbert. He only planned to. Before he could take his plan any further, someone else took Gilbert from us."

"No! Who would do such a thing?"

I took a heavy breath as I replied. "Do you want to explain or shall I? Gwen?"

Everyone turned to look at the sharp-dressed elf. Her eyes immediately widened behind her cat-shaped eyeglasses.

Gwen looked at me in horror. "Me...?"

I nodded – all the clues pointed at her.

I explained. "You were the inconspicuous elf sent by Elf Employment to work at Claus Cottage, or so you said. But you've been dodging calls since you arrived and insisted we shouldn't speak to your employers. Because you weren't sent here; even though you've been working hard all these years, so you'd be assigned here without anyone questioning it – you've always wanted to work here. But there was a problem: you couldn't work here if there wasn't a spot available for you. So, you kidnapped Gilbert."

"What... that's... that's ridiculous!" Gwen stammered as she squirmed in her seat. "I was *truly* just sent here by Elf Employment. I even showed you the contract when I got here!"

"Which was why we didn't suspect you," I answered. "You came here seamlessly – with the right paperwork and the perfect resume. No one would've guessed it was all planned."

"Because it wasn't!" Gwen argued, her face turning a shade of red. "The only reason I'm even in here is because you all said I was welcome! If I knew it would make me a suspect, I wouldn't have stayed."

At that point, Gwen jumped out of her seat. "In fact, I'm leaving. This is ridiculous."

"Sit back down," Mrs Claus commanded; even I almost fell to the nearest seat. No wonder Gwen quickly returned to her original position with wide eyes and quivering lips.

As Mrs Claus' eyes fell on Gwen, the elf grew teary and said, "I... I didn't do it, Mrs Claus. I swear! I left that morning when you said my services weren't needed. You know that! I'm only here because I collapsed in the snow trying to..."

"Trying to what?" Mrs Claus challenged.

Gwen looked down at her pointed red shoes and mumbled. "Trying to impress you... so you'd take me in."

"So, you took Gilbert instead?" Mrs Claus asked, hurt.

"I didn't!" Gwen remained firm. She turned to me with a glare. "How could you even come up with such an accusation, Holly! You don't even have evidence!"

Wiggles chimed in. "It's a fair point. Do you have evidence, Holly?"

"Of course," I answered confidently, striding towards the drawer near the front door where I had stored Gwen's resume. I pulled out the folder and returned to the group, showing everyone what it was. "The first piece of evidence is in here."

I handed it to Wiggles, who immediately opened the folder. Despite being seemingly unsure of what he was looking at, he passed it to Cornelius, who was also clueless. So, he passed it on to Nick, who passed it on to Mrs Claus.

Mrs Claus skimmed through the impressive resume. "What exactly am I looking at here, Holly?"

"The first clue that gave away Gwen's ill intentions – her calligraphy certification," I revealed. "The ever-intelligent Mitzy pointed out that most elves have similar handwriting because they get their certifications from the same academy. Gwen has a three-star mark on her calligraphy course."

August gasped in realisation. "Are you saying Gwen *copied* Gilbert's handwriting and made us believe that Gilbert left of his own volition?"

"Oh, come on!" Gwen threw an annoyed hand in the air. "That's a leap!"

"Is it?" I turned to Gwen. "Then I'm sure you wouldn't mind showing us your handwriting."

"That's counterintuitive – basically a setup! Like that elf said, most of us have similar handwriting! Maybe *she* copied Gilbert's handwriting!"

Father Christmas spoke. "I'll warn you not to speak about Mitzy like that. She would do no such thing."

Gwen held back a huff, unable to speak up against Father Christmas. Instead, she looked at me and crossed her arms. "Well, I refuse to show my handwriting since you'll incriminate me either way!"

"I'm not incriminating you; you did that to yourself when you kidnapped Gilbert." I breathed.

"But I didn't kidnap him," Gwen drawled.

At that point, Nick was getting tired of Gwen's banter, so

he pulled a photo from his jacket and slapped it on the table before Gwen. "Then, how would you explain this?"

Everyone looked closer to the photograph – it was a screen capture from one of Elf Employment's security cameras. Nick and I secured it prior to returning to Claus Cottage.

In the photo, you could see Gwen's small frame as she borrowed a black company vehicle at exactly 11:29pm on December 23 – sixteen minutes before Gilbert was last seen getting into a similar-looking vehicle.

Nick pointed a finger at the photo. "That's you, isn't it? You borrowed a company car on the night Gilbert disappeared."

Wiggles almost slid out of his seat as he moved closer and closer to the photo. He remarked. "This does look like the vehicle we saw Gilbert get in! How could we have missed this?"

"It's a new vehicle," I assured Wiggles. "Elf Employment was just about to register it once regular office hours resumed in Candy Cane Hollow. Hence, we didn't find it on record yet."

We all turned to Gwen for an answer.

Gwen's eyes were wide, almost guilty, but she still managed to come up with an excuse. "It's not a crime to borrow a car from your company! It was snowing hard that night! This doesn't prove anything."

Cornelius cleared his throat and pulled his heavy weight up from the settee. "Wiggles will stay here while I check this vehicle at Elf Employment for evidence. May I borrow a sleigh, Father Christmas?"

Father Christmas also stood up with a sour expression. "I'll fetch you one. Come on."

As they exited, Gwen felt pressure on her. The room was getting smaller as we closed in on her.

To get under her skin, I added. "I don't know how you did it, Gwen, but you also somehow knew Gilbert's cookware would play an important role in his kidnapping. So you left it on the driveway for Scraper to find it. You knew Scraper wouldn't be able to resist it; what you didn't think was that we would find it."

"Gilbert couldn't help boasting on ElfBook about those pans. He could be so annoying!"

Gwen's face was getting redder and redder by the second until, finally, she broke.

"Fine!" Gwen sputtered with tears in her eyes. "I did it! I took Gilbert away but only because I wanted to get close to you, Mrs Claus!"

The darkness in Mrs Claus' face eased a little. "What do you mean, Gwen?"

Crying, Gwen confessed. "You have been my inspiration since I met you at my orphanage all those years ago. When I met you again a few years ago, I decided it was fate that brought us together, so I've been working hard trying to get close to you. As an elf, I knew the highest honour I could have was to work for you here, but I've waited for years, and even when I was finally the best employee in Elf Employment, I still couldn't come here... all because of Gilbert!"

Gwen wailed like a child; tears, and snot all over her face as she did so.

Mrs Claus' angry heart quickly turned to compassion as she strode the room towards Gwen's side. "Oh my, Gwen, you shouldn't have taken it this far. Everyone, including you, is welcome here at Claus Cottage. You could've just walked in here and had a cup of tea with me! You didn't have to kidnap Gilbert."

"I'm sorry!" Gwen cried in Mrs Claus' arms for a moment. "I'm really sorry, Mrs Claus."

As Gwen cried, Wiggles sighed. "Well, this is awkward. I'll have to take you to Candy Cane Custody, Gwen."

"Not so quick, Wiggles," Mrs Claus raised a dismissive hand, making Gwen look up in adoration at Mrs Claus. But Mrs Claus stopped Wiggles not because she wanted to save Gwen from Candy Cane Custody. She turned to red-faced Gwen. "You have to take us to Gilbert first, Gwen. If I really mean that much to you, you'll bring us to him."

Sniffing, Gwen knew there was only one answer, so she nodded. "I'll take you to Gilbert."

## 24

Apart from the Frozen Flowering Forest, another one of Candy Cane Hollow's biggest mysteries was how four people and one elf could fit inside Wiggles' Fiat.

To ensure that Gwen wouldn't attempt to flee, Wiggles offered to drive us to Gilbert's location in his tiny car. He sat in the driver's seat while Nick rode shotgun. In the backseat, Gwen sat between Mrs Claus and me so she wouldn't try and jump out of the moving car.

We had been driving for eighteen repetitions of *Last Christmas* to a place I only knew was on the outskirts of Candy Cane Hollow. It was a rural city roughly an hour away.

No wonder Gwen had borrowed a company car to take Gilbert.

From the moment she confessed until about fifteen minutes ago, Gwen had been crying and apologising to Mrs Claus nonstop. Mrs Claus, being the kindhearted woman that she was, consoled Gwen and said she was already making amends by bringing them to Gilbert.

Gwen had assured us that she might've kidnapped Gilbert, but she never intended to hurt him, so he was safe. She, however, brought him to the poor outskirts of Candy Cane Hollow, where barely anyone had phones, televisions, or even public transportation.

It was a smart move – I'd give Gwen that. She cut off Gilbert from the rest of the world, so finding him would be a challenge. And it was indeed challenging. Now, I just wanted it to be over with.

I just wanted to see Gilbert again.

As *Last Christmas* crawled and buried its way into my brain in some kind of endless musical torture, Gwen sniffed. "Are we really going to listen to the same tune the entire time?"

Wiggles continued singing to his favourite song, unbothered by Gwen's remark.

Folded into the cramped space in the backseat, I replied. "It's Wiggles' car, so it's his music."

"Feeling better now, dear?" Mrs Claus asked with care. Not for the first time, I was amazed by how kind and generous her spirit was.

"I am, thank you, Mrs Claus." Gwen wiped her cheeks with her coat sleeve.

For a while now, we had seen nothing but a stretch of snowy plains and a line of snow-covered pine trees under the dusk sky. But up ahead, we finally saw the first sign of this rural city—a run-down street sign that read: *Welcome to Pine Creek!*

The letters were barely readable because of how weathered the sign was.

"We're here," Nick said as the yellow Fiat sped past the sign and along a road with winding tree branches and endless pine needles on the road.

Soon, the ramshackle town of Pine Creek welcomed us with curling smoke from old-fashioned chimneys and small log homes lining both sides of the road. By log homes, I didn't mean log *cabins* – I meant generation-old wood, peeling paint, and stretches of clotheslines beside and behind every modest home.

It was evident it was a place for people on low incomes. There were no fancy cars or grand buildings. Nonetheless, it was lively and decent and clear that the families who called the place home were doing all they could to make their homes and gardens look well-presented and festive.

We passed by a house with an old tire for a swing, hand-me-down toys that children played with, and repurposed tools for decorations. Christmas lights were lit from within coloured bottles, and old quilts were used as banners.

"How did you even think of bringing Gilbert to this place?" Mrs Claus asked out of curiosity and concern.

"It's where I live. I came here after I left the orphanage," Gwen said with a sense of pride – the kind of dignity that came with having made it on her own.

Looking around the place closer, we saw people gathered over a shared bonfire and children laughed as they ran around and chased each other. It seemed like it didn't matter that Gwen didn't have a family of her own – she had had a community.

"Where to, Gwen?" Wiggles asked.

"Just go straight," Gwen instructed. "You'll see an apartment complex called Yule Apartments. You won't miss it."

And just like Gwen said, a mile later, we saw a four-storey wooden building.

*Yule Apartments,* the sign hanging from the entrance read.

Wiggles pulled over right across the building. "Do you need me to come with you, Mrs Claus?"

Mrs Claus pushed the car door open. "No need, Wiggles. Rest up for now. A party of four will be enough to fetch Gilbert."

Except for Wiggles, all of us alighted the vehicle. Gwen took a deep breath, giving her lungs a whiff of smoke and pine. "It's this way."

As soon as we were out of the vehicle, everyone turned to look at us. People and elves stopped what they were doing to stare. Curtains twitched as people inside the buildings sneaked glances at us. The entire place went silent as we passed.

Nick stayed behind Mrs Claus and me. We followed Gwen into the building, which had narrow hallways made from stripped pinewood.

There were numbers on each apartment door, and the doors were spaced close enough together that it was clear the apartments were compact. The hallway echoed with laughter, conversation, and even the sound of kitchenware as they prepared dinner.

"It's on the second floor," Gwen said, leading the way.

We climbed a flight of stairs, and the same narrow hallway squeezed us. When we got to Room 2-C, Gwen paused and retrieved her key from her coat pocket.

Suddenly, I felt nervous.

I had no idea what Gilbert would look like – he had been here for days, all on his own, unless Gwen had an accomplice inside keeping an eye on him.

Gwen pushed the door open, revealing a simple studio apartment wide enough for two people to live in. A bit smaller than my old London apartment, but otherwise pretty much the same. A bed by the window, a table at the other end of the bed, a bathroom on the corner, and a kitchen right by the entrance. It was clean. No figurine was out of place.

But no Gilbert in sight.

"Oh boy," Gwen quietly exclaimed. "Looks like Gilbert has been keeping busy."

Mrs Claus looked around with concern. "What do you mean by that? Why isn't he here?"

"Oh, he's here," Gwen nodded with certainty. "Let's just say I made it hard for him to leave. Wait here."

Mrs Claus glanced at me with slight fear, so I stepped up. "I'll come with you."

Gwen instantly knew why, but she held back a sigh. "Of course, I might run away. Follow me, then."

I nodded at Nick and Mrs Claus as I tailed Gwen closely to a nearby apartment. She knocked on the door, and an elf immediately came to get it.

Gwen spoke. "Have you seen Gilbert?"

"Your new boyfriend?" The female elf teased, giving me a funny look. "He's been cleaning apartments nonstop since he got here. He's probably on the third floor by now."

Cleaning apartments nonstop sounded like something Gilbert would do. No wonder the hallways were free from dust, dirt, and debris despite how crowded it was.

We headed up to the third floor; the strong smell of onion and beef made me wiggle my nose.

Gwen knocked on the first door, asking for Gilbert. She was led next door. We tried the next apartment. Again, we were pointed to the next door. We knocked on the third apartment, and finally, I heard a familiar voice coming from the other side.

"Coming!" *He* said.

I found myself crossing my fingers in wishful thinking as

the familiar voice scolded a bunch of laughing kids from inside the apartment.

The quick footsteps from the other side of the door came closer and closer.

*Please, please, please. Please be Gilbert.*

My eyes were hyper-focused on the door as the rusty doorknob turned and the creaking door slowly pulled open.

Behind it, a small and familiar figure in green pyjamas two sizes too big for him greeted us. "Finally, you're back –"

*Gilbert.*

Gilbert's eyes popped as he saw me standing behind Gwen. For a moment, neither of us knew what to do.

Gilbert's expression changed, and I was ready to get to my knees and give him the biggest embrace of his life, but then he deadpanned. "What are you doing in Pine Creek, Holly?"

WHILE MY REUNION with Gilbert was unceremonious, his and Mrs Claus' reunion wasn't.

As soon as we walked into Gwen's apartment, Mrs Claus strode towards Gilbert, bent down, and gave him the biggest embrace of his life.

I could see Mrs Claus getting teary-eyed as she was finally able to hug Gilbert – he was okay. He was safe.

Mrs Claus pulled away to check Gilbert. "Are you hurt?"

"Uh, no," Gilbert said casually as if he hadn't been missing for over three days. "However, I'm baffled why all of you are in Pine Creek, acting like... you've all missed me."

"What do you mean?" Mrs Claus acted offended by Gilbert's sentiments.

Gilbert glanced at Gwen questioningly while Gwen

looked away. He said. "Well, Gwen informed me that I had been sent on a special Christmas mission over here at Pine Creek – she said you sent for her, Mrs Claus."

By now, we were finally piecing everything together.

Gilbert had no idea we had almost lost our noggins trying to find him! To him, Mrs Claus just sent him here. To us, Gilbert was *supposed* to look like he ran away.

Gwen had really thought this plan through. I was almost impressed.

Mrs Claus let out a long, overdue sigh. "Goodness gumdrops, Gilbert! Didn't you ever wonder why I would suddenly send you on a Christmas mission out of the blue? And without discussing it with you first?"

I did wonder," Gilbert paused to think, realising he had also been duped. He gasped and jabbed a finger at Gwen. "You... what did you do!?"

Gwen ran behind me to hide. "You have to understand; I only did it because I wanted to work at Claus Cottage!"

Gilbert stomped his way towards Gwen. In no time, both of them were circling around me.

"So, you kidnapped me?" Gilbert screeched.

"You got in the car on your own!" Gwen argued as she ran in circles.

"Only because you said Mrs Claus sent you to pick me up and drive me over here to share Christmas joy with this community!"

"And you did share Christmas joy!"

By now, Gilbert was trying to catch Gwen, but she was hopping furniture in the small apartment and dodging Gilbert's advances.

"You tried to rob me of my job and my home!" Gilbert was furious, as the realisation of Gwen's true plan sank in. "How long were you planning on keeping me here?"

"Erm, until they forgot about you...? I figured at some point they'd have to replace you." Gwen replied with honesty.

Gilbert screamed like a madman, running for Gwen at full speed, but Nick got in between them. "Okay, calm down, Gilbert!"

Still, Gilbert resisted Nick's hold. "I swear, I will... I will hang you like mistletoe, Gwen!"

"That's enough, Gilbert," Mrs Claus said.

Gilbert jumped back from Nick and shrugged. "I'm sorry, Mrs Claus, but this is unacceptable. I am just learning that I have been fooled! I've been cleaning apartments and cooking meals day in and day out since I got here! And for what? So someone could steal my place at Claus Cottage?"

"Do you really think we would let that happen, Gilbert?" I asked, raising my eyebrows at him.

Gilbert frowned. "I don't know! It took you three days to get me, so maybe!"

"They didn't," Gwen chimed. "Even with my credentials, they wouldn't let me touch your things or move stuff in your kitchen!"

"You've been in my kitchen?!" Gilbert was about to pounce again.

Thankfully, Mrs Claus said. "What Gwen is trying to say is that you are irreplaceable, Gilbert. You have no idea how far we looked for you, most especially Holly. She worried about you all day and all night."

Gilbert looked up at me with teary eyes and pouting lips. "You did?"

"Well, I kept forgetting to mix my hot chocolate with milk instead of water," I teased. "No one was there to remind me."

Suddenly, Gilbert ran towards me and hugged me. "Thank you, Holly! I appreciate it!"

I patted Gilbert's hair. "I'm just glad you're okay."

Gilbert pulled away as he wiped the bottom of his eyes. "What happens now?"

Nick opened the curtain to show Gilbert Wiggles' yellow Fiat. "We take you home, and, well, Gwen will be taken to Candy Cane Custody."

Gilbert nodded intently. "As she should be."

"Oh, come on!" Gwen exclaimed. "You can't tell me you didn't enjoy your time here at Yule Apartments."

"It doesn't matter if I did," Gilbert argued. "You brought me here with ill intentions!"

"But you did enjoy being here?" Mrs Claus asked.

Gilbert looked at Mrs Claus guiltily. "Well, it felt good to make warm meals and help keep homes clean for the families here. Although I was confused why I was sent here at first, after a day, I realised this was something you'd want me to do, Mrs Claus – let more people experience Claus hospitality."

I watched Mrs Claus' face soften and pull into a sweet smile. "Oh, Gilbert. If you say it like that, I might just make you stay here."

Gilbert shook his head a few times. "No, Mrs Claus. Not forever."

"For a while?" Mrs Claus joked.

Gilbert grew serious. "If I can. I just mean, there are a few more apartments upstairs I have to clean and make meals for. I already did it for the other families, so it wouldn't be right if I didn't finish it."

"Of course," Mrs Claus smiled. "You should finish this beautiful thing *you* started, Gilbert. We'll wait for you."

Gilbert's face lit up. I could tell he really had had a good time helping other people. So, I suggested. "Maybe we can even make something like this a new Claus Christmas tradition. What do you think, Mrs Claus?"

Mrs Claus clapped her hands. "A wonderful idea, Holly! Like Gilbert said, everyone should experience Claus hospitality! You and I will take charge of planning this, Holly."

I nodded, mirroring Mrs Claus' warm smile that I hadn't seen in a few days.

"Maybe we could all pitch in. I wouldn't mind helping with some of the cleaning," I volunteered.

Mrs Claus looked at me with wide eyes full of warning, but I realised my mistake too late.

"Is my cleaning not good enough for you, Holly? Is that it? Do you think you can do a better job? Why, I've a good mind to hang up my..." Gilbert began, but before he could finish his outraged words, I grabbed him in a hug so tight it knocked the air out of him.

"It's so good to have you back," I said, and I meant every word.

## 25

"Whoever committed the mortal sin of washing these plates?"

"Who put the cayenne powder here?"

"Who thought cherry tomatoes and strawberries should go on the same tray?"

Poor Gilbert found himself complaining about everything wrong in his kitchen after being gone for more than three days.

It was his first order of business as soon as he arrived at Claus Cottage; he didn't even notice Patrice and Ginger hiding in the den to surprise him as he raced through the house to the kitchen.

The welcoming committee took no offence to Gilbert unknowingly ignoring them. If anything, they laughed as they followed all of us down the hallway to watch Gilbert organise *his* kitchen.

Mrs Claus had a beautiful smile on her face as she gazed at Gilbert lovingly – like a mother would to her prodigal son. It was no secret Mrs Claus considered Gilbert to be part of her family.

"He's back, all right," Ginger nudged me playfully as she stood next to me, a frantic Gilbert pacing around the kitchen and putting things back into place.

I smiled sincerely, my entire body releasing the tension in my muscles built of concern and regret in the last few days. "I'm glad he's safe."

Patrice let out a long sigh of relief. "Who did you say took him again?"

I pulled her back to the den since I didn't want to upset Gilbert all over again by reminding him about Gwen. With Ginger behind us, I said. "It's Gwen – the elf who came here as Gilbert's replacement."

Ginger crossed her arms. "Let me guess, she wanted to be Claus Cottage's next house elf?"

"Yes, she adored Mrs Claus that much," I replied.

"Oh, Mrs Claus' kindness can be such a blessing and a curse." Patrice breathed sadly. "If you're too kind, people take it as a sign of encouragement to get close. Too close."

"Encouragement to kidnap another elf?" Ginger pointed out. "Kindness should never be an excuse to do that. Imagine what Gilbert went through!"

"A lot of cleaning and cooking, actually..." I answered, garnering looks of confusion from the group. So, I explained. "Gwen told Gilbert that Mrs Claus sent him to Pine Creek to help out the community there. You can imagine how seriously Gilbert took that!"

"So, he didn't even know he had been kidnapped?" Patrice asked.

"That's a good thing, right?" I responded. "At least he didn't think he was in grave danger the entire time."

"That sounds more concerning..." Patrice shuddered. "Imagine having a kidnapper who was so cunning you didn't even know you had been kidnapped!"

"So, what's going to happen to Gwen?" Ginger enquired.

"She's been taken by Wiggles to Candy Cane Custody. Wiggles said she'll be staying at a...standard room." I wasn't sure what that meant, but I could still recall how calm Gwen was when Wiggles asked her to squeeze into his Fiat.

The elf showed no fear or panic, only regret.

It was Ginger's turn to shudder. "A standard room? That's terrible!"

Now I wish I had read the pamphlet for Candy Cane Custody in more detail. "Is that a bad thing? I thought Candy Cane Custody is pretty much a hotel, except you can't leave the premises."

"Pretty much a hotel until you get booked at a standard room—it means you get the worst view, a bathroom with no bathtub just a shower, and three-course meals instead of five!"

"They give three-course meals at Candy Cane Custody?"

"Only to the worst offenders," Ginger shook her head sadly.

"What did she expect after she committed a crime against the Clauses," Patrice nodded to herself.

Before I could react, August suddenly came running down the stairs. "Is it true? Is Gilbert home?"

"Yeah –"

August didn't even give me a chance to finish; she bolted straight to the kitchen with teary eyes as I heard her shout. "Gilbert!"

In a short amount of time, August and Gilbert had developed a friendship over their shared dedication to house chores and both of them delighted in their constant disagreements about the best way to cook and bake.

I allowed myself a smile. Gilbert was safely back home,

and it was clear he was loved. He was a vital part of the Claus family.

We heard Gilbert squeal as August probably put him in a hug that might border a chokehold, but by the time I peeked into the kitchen, Gilbert had given in and hugged August back. "There, there. Now you don't have to mess with my kitchen."

August pulled back with a tear and a laugh. "It wasn't just me – it was also Holly, who *still* kept making her hot chocolates with hot water."

Gilbert's eyes flew right onto me like daggers flying across the room. He clicked his tongue. "When will you ever learn that hot chocolates are made with warm milk, Holly?"

Smiling sheepishly, I changed the subject. "Did you notice that Ginger and Patrice brought cake?"

"Welcome home banners, too!" Patrice chimed behind me.

While Gilbert could see what I was trying to do, he simply shook his head and chuckled. "I did notice those; I just couldn't wait another second to see what kind of a mess everyone left my kitchen in! But, really, I appreciate it, everyone."

Gilbert, always the drama queen, climbed a stool, brought a wooden spatula to his mouth as a microphone, and began his speech. "Although I am offended that Patrice and Ginger thought a store-bought cake would be better than the ones I bake, I am grateful for the sentiments. In fact, I am grateful for all of you. For everything you did to bring me home..."

He sighed dramatically, pretending to pat a non-existent tear from the bottom of his eyes. "In return, my service and loyalty will forever be to this house – to the Clauses. I couldn't be any luckier than I already am, to be a part of this wonderful home."

I swore I saw Mrs Claus wipe a *real* tear from her eyes before they fell, but she clapped her hand and instructed Gilbert. "Get down from the stool, Gilbert! Where are your manners? We have guests!"

Gilbert gritted his teeth together in slight embarrassment, quickly hopping down the stool. "Right away, Mrs Claus!"

Mrs Claus chuckled. "If you're so grateful for all of us, how about we all make another Christmas dinner? We'd love to have one with you at the table."

We all clapped and cheered our enthusiasm for this suggestion. Mrs Claus always came up with the best and most heartwarming ideas.

Gilbert's face brightened, his cheeks blushing pink. "Well, I have to admit I was a little bit busy making dinner for the residents of Yule Logs on Christmas Eve..."

"Good, because we'd love to have another Christmas dinner." Mrs Claus looked around the room. "Isn't that right, everyone?"

It wasn't even a question that needed to be asked – we all knew Gilbert belonged at our table, and since he wasn't with us on Christmas Eve, it was only fitting we held another one with him.

While traditions were nice, certain rules didn't apply. If the Clauses wished to have another Christmas dinner on the 26th of December, then it should happen.

A chorus of agreement could be heard in the room.

August automatically stepped forward, only to be shot down by Gilbert. "I'll help!"

"No, you won't!" Gilbert said firmly. "All of you should

just sit tight and wait. I'll whip up a great meal in an hour. Trust me!"

Finally, Claus Cottage felt complete.

While Gilbert worked on cooking dinner, the rest of us gathered in the den to play *Monopoly* – of course, it was Christmas-themed.

A fire cackled from the fireplace, biscuits with dips never ran out, and everyone seemed to be having fun. Even Jeb, who was now crawling on the carpet, seemed to recognise that something special was happening.

As promised, Gilbert came through with his one-hour deadline. Impressive, as always.

Whatever Christmas magic he pulled, Gilbert had successfully prepared a cheese board, bouillabaisse, endive salad, and scalloped potatoes. As he laid them all on the table, he remarked. "I thought the cake Patrice and Ginger bought would be a waste if I made another dessert..."

"Are you sure it's not because you didn't have enough time to prepare everything?" Ginger quipped.

Gilbert tried not to look guilty as he sat and joined us. "I was being considerate!"

"Of course you were," Ginger winked.

Gilbert huffed as he put a napkin over his lap; we all laughed.

Although we were two nights late for the Christmas Eve dinner, I felt blessed to still have a proper one – this time with Gilbert.

Looking around the table, I watched each person basking in their own joy.

Father Christmas scooped a bowl full of bouillabaisse for him and Mrs Claus. Mrs Claus thoughtfully handed Gilbert a slice of cake. August, Tom, and Jeb looked like such a perfect happy family it was like they had come straight from a TV commercial. Ginger groaned with satisfaction as she tasted the endive salad. Patrice chatted with her cousin.

Then, there was Nick... sliding his hand under the table to hold my hand. Smiling at me, he whispered. "Merry Christmas *again,* Holly."

I smiled back at him. "Merry Christmas, too, Nick."

SNOW FELL, settled, and shimmered across the white blanket already spread across the lawn. A quarter before midnight, and even then, the world of Candy Cane Hollow looked alive with all the blinking lights at every home and tree.

The world was quiet; the festivity was almost over, my glass of red wine half-empty as I stood outside waiting for Nick to return with a thicker coat.

As I hugged myself against the cold, I could hear faint laughter travelling out from the den. Gilbert, Ginger, and Patrice continued sharing a bottle of wine.

Father Christmas and Mrs Claus had excused themselves to bed over an hour ago. Mrs Claus' exhaustion finally seeped into her body now that she was allowed to relax.

Over the dinner, we had discussed Ethan Evergreen and the future of his store. Nick felt confident that there were contracts he could offer to Evergreen Emporium to help with the running of Santa HQ. It seemed the business could be saved, after all.

As for Nick and I, he had asked me to meet him on the front lawn to talk.

If it wasn't for the ring on my finger, I might think he was going to propose – this was the perfect night to do it. Again. I laughed at myself for being a new romantic. Before Nick, I wouldn't even be caught looking at engagement rings on a private tab on my phone. Yet here I was, imagining a second proposal from Santa himself.

"Here you go," Nick's voice echoed behind me as he carefully placed one of his coats over my shoulders. "I wouldn't want you to catch a cold."

"That's alright; I could trust Gilbert to make me some warm honey lemon tea every night until I was better," I smiled.

"Says Dr. Holly Wood," Nick pulled me close with one arm. He looked out into the world and let out an exhale. "It's always the quiet parts of nights like this that make me sentimental."

I leaned into Nick's warmth. "I know what you mean. Gilbert's disappearance and return makes me sentimental, too. For a moment there, I thought we wouldn't see him again."

"You only thought – you didn't believe it," Nick remarked with a hint of adoration in his voice. "You refused to give up on him even when it looked as if he had chosen to leave."

"Because he wouldn't do that."

"I know that so much better now," Nick admitted. "And almost losing Gilbert made me realise how we shouldn't take people for granted just because we already have them."

"You're not taking me for granted," I pinpointed with a smile.

"Maybe..."

As the twinkling lights cast dancing shadows across the garden, I turned to Nick and put a hand over his chest.

"Why did you really want to talk out here, Nick? Is there something you want to say?"

Nick had a soft look in his eyes, almost like I was the one who had gone missing and just returned – he looked at me like he had been searching for me. For his whole life, maybe. "Because I've been watching you all night, Holly, and I can't help but wonder how I got so lucky to be engaged to someone so loving and thoughtful as you."

I felt flowers bloom right out of my ribs. "Nick... what are you doing? You *already* proposed."

"I know," Nick chuckled. "Frankly, you deserve a hundred proposals and a thousand engagement rings, but even those wouldn't be enough. Because what you deserve is a husband."

I blinked at Nick, unsure where the conversation was headed. But as clueless as I was, my heart beat like crazy. Forget butterflies.

Nick continued. "So, I've been thinking, let's not wait it out any longer. Let's get married, Holly. Right after New Year. Let's just do it – let's dive into married life together."

I stared at Nick agog. For a moment, I didn't know what to say. I was both suddenly excited and in disbelief. "I, uh... I'd love to get married to you right away, Nick, but that's, what, six days from now?"

I'd heard stories of brides losing their heads when preparing for their wedding. Imagine doing it all in just six days. And yet, I liked the idea. I was up for the challenge.

Nick took the glass of wine from my hand and set it aside on the wall. Then, he took my hands in his. "I know it's overwhelming, but with August, my mum, and everybody else, we have an entire team behind us. We'll nail your dream wedding in six days."

There was no way I would've believed Nick if he wasn't

Santa – if I wasn't in a literal Christmas wonderland, where flowers freeze in the spring and reindeer talk. There were one too many impossible things happening around me. So, pulling off my dream wedding in six days wasn't nearly as impossible as everything else.

"So?" Nick was clearly a little nervous about my silence.

Finally, I let out a deep breath. "Yes, Nick, let's get married in six days."

Nick let out the shakiest, most satisfied sigh I had ever heard, then pulled me into a tight embrace. "Yes! Yes! Thank you, Holly! You won't regret it."

"I sure won't –" My words got caught up in my throat as bright lights suddenly emerged from the sky.

The words 'we're getting hitched' slowly spelled out into the star-filled sky.

"Nick!" I scolded him playfully. "Did you seriously put on a light show for this?"

Just then, people cheered and clapped from behind us. When I turned, Father Christmas, Mrs Claus, August, Tom, Jeb, Gilbert, Ginger, and Patrice were all peering out from the den windows and raising a glass to us.

I turned to Nick, who shrugged his shoulders. "Would you believe I asked Patrice to pull this together just twenty minutes ago? See what we can accomplish?"

I laughed in disbelief, glancing at the dancing lights in the sky. "Well, you proved a point."

"Kiss her! Kiss her! Kiss her!" The group – led by Mrs Claus, of course - chanted like we were in high school.

It only made me laugh harder, but seeing how happy everyone was for us, I didn't want to let them down. So, I moved closer to Nick, stood on my tiptoes, and kissed him on the lips.

In six days, I was officially going to be Mrs Claus-in-training.

## THE END

## PRE-ORDER THE NEXT BOOK:
### HOLLY JOLLY HOMICIDE

## 26

# CHESTNUT, BACON & CHIVE SOUP

C hestnut, Bacon, and Chive Soup with Carrot, Celery, Leek, and Shallots
**Ingredients:**

- 200g cooked chestnuts (vacuum-packed or canned)
- 150g bacon, chopped
- 2 tablespoons olive oil or butter
- 2 medium carrots, peeled and diced
- 2 celery stalks, diced
- 1 leek, cleaned and sliced
- 4 shallots, finely chopped
- 2 garlic cloves, minced
- 1 litre chicken or vegetable broth
- 1 teaspoon fresh thyme leaves (optional)
- 1 bay leaf
- 1/2 teaspoon ground nutmeg
- Salt and pepper to taste
- 200ml heavy cream or milk (optional for a creamy version)

- 2 tablespoons chopped fresh chives
- Crusty bread, for serving

**INSTRUCTIONS:**

1. **Prepare the Ingredients:**
2. Dice the carrots, celery, leek, and shallots.
3. Chop the bacon into small pieces.
4. Roughly chop the chestnuts if they are whole.
5. **Cook the Bacon:**
6. In a large pot or Dutch oven, heat the olive oil or butter over medium heat.
7. Add the chopped bacon and cook until crispy. Remove the bacon with a slotted spoon and set aside, leaving the rendered fat in the pot.
8. **Sauté the Vegetables:**
9. Add the diced carrots, celery, leek, and shallots to the pot.
10. Sauté for about 5-7 minutes, until the vegetables start to soften.
11. Add the minced garlic and cook for another minute.
12. **Add Chestnuts and Broth:**
13. Add the chopped chestnuts to the pot, stirring to combine with the vegetables.
14. Pour in the chicken or vegetable broth.
15. Add the thyme (if using), bay leaf, and ground nutmeg.
16. Season with salt and pepper to taste.
17. **Simmer the Soup:**

18. Bring the mixture to a boil, then reduce the heat to low and let it simmer for about 20-25 minutes, until the vegetables are tender and the flavours are well combined.
19. **Blend the Soup:**
20. Remove the bay leaf.
21. Using an immersion blender, blend the soup until smooth. Alternatively, you can blend the soup in batches using a regular blender. Be careful with hot liquids.
22. **Add Cream (Optional):**
23. If you prefer a creamy soup, stir in the heavy cream or milk.
24. Return the soup to a gentle simmer for a few minutes.
25. **Finish and Serve:**
26. Stir in the crispy bacon and chopped chives.
27. Taste and adjust seasoning with more salt, pepper, or nutmeg if needed.
28. Ladle the soup into bowls and garnish with extra chives and bacon if desired.
29. Serve hot with crusty bread on the side.

ENJOY YOUR DELICIOUS CHESTNUT, bacon, and chive soup!

# ABOUT THE AUTHOR

Mona Marple is a lover of all things book-related. When she isn't working on her next release, she's probably curled up somewhere warm reading a good story.

Mona is a fan of all things festive and is looking forward to adding to the Christmas Cozy Mystery series over the years. Her other cozy mysteries include the Waterfell Tweed series, the Mystic Springs paranormal series and the Mexican Mysteries series.

Mona lives in Nottinghamshire, England with her bread baking husband, her always-singing daughter, and their pampered Labradoodle, Coco. In fact, Mona's online reader group were a big part of persuading Mona's husband to welcome Coco into their home!

Stay up to date with her latest news by joining her eMail list at http://www.monamarple.com/vip-readers

www.ingramcontent.com/pod-product-compliance
Lightning Source LLC
Chambersburg PA
CBHW020119150725
29622CB00011B/493